When she looked across at him he was laughing, dark eyes warm and tender in the face that she knew as well as her own.

And then he was on his feet and coming towards her, and Francine knew if she didn't stop him now it would be too late. They would make love, and the bliss of it would be wiped out by a feeling of bitter sweetness because it could be the last time.

So why was she holding out her arms to him, throwing off the covers and letting him slip the straps of her nightdress off her shoulders?

'It's been so long, Francine,' he said as he caressed her from top to toe. 'We can't go on like this. I haven't stopped loving you for a second, in spite of the arguments and misunderstandings, and I pray that you feel the same about me.'

'Yes, I do.'

Dear Reader

Welcome to the second of my books where coast and countryside combine to bring you the beautiful Devon village of *Bluebell Cove*. A place where doctors and nurses in the medical practice look after the health of the local folk and share their joys and sorrows, and in return have the respect and support of their patients when it is their turn to need a friend.

I live in a village in the Cheshire countryside myself, and it never ceases to amaze me how close is the bond between those who live here. When one of them hurts they all hurt. When one of them rejoices they all rejoice.

In CHRISTMAS IN BLUEBELL COVE, GP Ethan and his lovely French wife Francine discover that a Bluebell Cove Christmas, surrounded by the love of this warm community, is all that's really needed to help them understand how to love each other and mend their marriage so that they can enjoy their lovely little family.

If you have enjoyed reading about the folks there, do look out for the next in this series THE VILLAGE NURSE'S HAPPY-EVER-AFTER also available this month. Book four will be coming along shortly.

So do let's keep in touch, dear reader, as I write and you read about golden beaches, clotted cream teas, and *romance* in Devon—glorious Devon!

Abigail Gordon

CHRISTMAS IN BLUEBELL COVE

BY
ABIGAIL GORDON

First published in Great Britain 2010
by Mills & Boon,
an imprint of Harlequin (UK) Limited,
Large Print edition 2011
Eton House, 18-24 Paradise Road,
Richmond, Surrey TW9 1SR

© Abigail Gordon 2010

ISBN: 978 0 263 21736 0

Harlequin (UK) policy is to use papers that are natural, renewable and recyclable products and made from wood grown in sustainable forests. The logging and manufacturing process conform to the legal environmental regulations of the country of origin.

Printed and bound in Great Britain
by CPI Antony Rowe, Chippenham, Wiltshire

Abigail Gordon loves to write about the fascinating combination of medicine and romance from her home in a Cheshire village. She is active in local affairs, and is even called upon to write the script for the annual village pantomime! Her eldest son is a hospital manager, and helps with all her medical research. As part of a close-knit family, she treasures having two of her sons living close by, and the third one not too far away. This also gives her the added pleasure of being able to watch her delightful grandchildren growing up.

Recent titles by the same author:

WEDDING BELLS FOR THE VILLAGE NURSE†
THE VILLAGE NURSE'S HAPPY-EVER-AFTER†
COUNTRY MIDWIFE, CHRISTMAS BRIDE*
A SUMMER WEDDING AT WILLOWMERE*
A BABY FOR THE VILLAGE DOCTOR*
CHRISTMAS AT WILLOWMERE*

The Willowmere Village Stories
†*The Bluebell Cove Stories*

CHAPTER ONE

IT HAD been a mistake coming back to Bluebell Cove for Christmas, Francine Lomax thought as she stood on the snow-covered path of the house that she hadn't set foot in for months.

When she unlocked the door there was silence inside, no one to greet her, which wasn't surprising as they hadn't known she was coming. She bent and picked up a trainer left lying in the middle of the hall, putting it into a nearby cupboard. Then she gathered together the last delivery of mail before Christmas which was lying behind the door, and placed it on the hall table in a neat pile. There was a letter from Ethan's solicitor amongst it and her insides trembled at its implications.

A doll belonging to Kirstie was sitting upright on the bottom step of the stairs and the choking feeling that she kept getting was back. It was all so familiar, yet she felt like a stranger in her own home.

Her baggage was still outside in the hire car that she'd picked up at the airport, and as she went to bring it in Francine was aware that there was music and laughter coming from somewhere not too far away, the sound of people enjoying themselves.

There might be silence in the house, but there were those out there who were making the most of the festive season and she was reminded of the vow she'd made to herself not to put the blight on the children's Christmas by arriving without warning and bringing her melancholy with her.

When she'd carried her suitcases upstairs she put them in the spare room where she would be sleeping and then went down again to await the arrival of her husband and children.

She'd been missing Ben and Kirstie dreadfully and their father too because it had been so much longer since she'd seen *him,* but she had

only herself to blame for that. The last thing
Ethan had wanted was for her to go stomping
off to live in Paris, in contrast to being just a
frequent visitor as had been the case when her
parents had been alive, and as Christmas had approached she'd begun to wish she hadn't agreed
to the children coming back to Bluebell Cove
so early to spend it with their father.

Yet that was how it was going to have to be
because of the rift between Ethan and herself
that was getting wider all the time, so wide that
the divorce she'd asked for was under way with
wheels slowly turning in the background.

Bitterness had soured a marriage that had been
happy and fulfilling until she'd lost her parents
tragically in a coach crash while they had been
holidaying in the Balkans. As a result she had
inherited her childhood home in France, and
ever since had been desperate to live there.

The marriage might have stood a better chance
if tiny cracks hadn't already been appearing in it
ever since Ethan had taken over as head of The
Tides Medical Practice that cared for the health

and well-being of the inhabitants of Bluebell Cove. He had seemed prepared to put his commitment to his new position before everything else.

His acceptance of the responsibility had come about because of the early retirement due to poor health of the woman who had given her life to the practice and had felt that Ethan was the only person she could trust to continue the work there to the same high standards as herself.

But the niggles that had sometimes arisen because of that had been as nothing compared to his reaction to the heart-breaking homesickness that had overtaken her at the loss of her parents and swept her into the situation that now existed between them. So if the revellers out there were full of the Christmas spirit, *she* wasn't.

She could still hear the music somewhere nearby and supposed it was possible that her family might be involved in whatever was happening out there on a snowy Christmas Eve.

Snuggling back into the winter coat that she'd travelled in and zipping up fashionable boots that had the stamp of Paris on them, she decided to go and see what was taking place in the direction of the square where a big spruce that was decorated and illuminated every year at Christmas time.

Standing in the shadows, she saw that those present were lined up in pairs behind a man and woman who looked as if they were dressed as bride and groom.

It was odd, to say the least, but sure enough Ethan and the children were there with Kirstie and Ben partnering each other for what was about to take place, her daughter bright eyed and excited in a stylish pink dress that she hadn't seen before, and her son ill at ease.

Ethan was partnering a tall slender girl with brown hair, brown eyes and very pale skin. The last time Francine had seen Phoebe Howard she'd been pregnant, facing up nervously to the prospect of becoming a single mother, but she looked happy enough at the moment.

He was looking down at her, smiling at something she'd said, and Francine thought that if

Ethan was finding comfort in the arms of another woman it wasn't surprising. He'd had no joy in hers for many long months.

Neither he nor the children had noticed her, they were too engrossed in the moment, and she continued to stay out of sight, registering as she did so that the smiling bride was Jenna Balfour, the daughter of the woman who had been in charge of the village medical practice before Ethan had taken over. Incredibly her bridegroom was Lucas Devereux, of all people, her husband's closest friend.

At that moment the local school's band struck up and the two of them began to dance through the village in the direction of the headland overlooking the sea, with the rest of the revellers following behind.

Tears pricked Francine's eyes. She'd been happy here for twelve years with Ethan and the children as they'd come along. Bluebell Cove was a beautiful place with countryside in abundance and the mighty Atlantic close by.

But ever since she'd inherited the house in

France it had been *there* that she wanted to be, and although Ethan had understood, it hadn't stopped him from reminding her frequently that he'd just taken on a huge commitment by becoming senior partner in the village practice.

That he owed it to Barbara Balfour to keep the faith. In other words, he didn't intend to leave Bluebell Cove and move to France on the sudden whim of his grieving wife.

There had been no hint of what was to come on his part when she'd first suggested it. He'd been reasonable and understanding, promising they would have lots of holidays there. But as the months had gone by she hadn't changed her mind about living there permanently, insisting he owed her that because hadn't she spent twelve years in Bluebell Cove for his sake?

In the end he'd wearied of being told he was selfish and after one more heated exchange of words she'd gone, taking the children with her.

That had really tipped the balance of Ethan's patience and concern. He loved them just as much as she did, he'd told her coldly, would expect to see them regularly, and all her hopes that he might relent and follow them had turned out to be futile.

For Kirstie and Ben there'd been no problem. They'd always liked visiting their grandparents in France, and as their parents had kept their disenchantment with each other from them as much as possible, going to live in the charming house on the outskirts of Paris had been an exciting interlude in their lives.

They'd settled in at the school where she'd enrolled them without any problems, having picked up the language over the years on their visits to their grandparents, and life would have been perfect if only Ethan had been there with them.

The headland was graced by another huge Christmas tree and those at the front of the line of dancers had already whirled around it and were on their way back to where they'd started from, which meant that in a very short time her family was going to become aware of her presence.

Kirstie was the first to see her as she and Ben drew near, and her delighted cry of '*Maman*!' stopped her husband in his tracks and brought her children out of the ranks and into her waiting arms.

She could see above their heads that Ethan had started dancing again and was almost out of sight without even greeting her. Maybe it was to remind her that their life together was coming to its close, that she'd got what she wanted, a return to her roots that he wasn't going to be part of.

When she looked up he was observing her above the heads of the now dispersing dancers and the choking feeling was there again. He was still the only man who made her pulse leap, with hair dark and crisply curling and eyes blue as the sea on a summer day as its tides came and went on the sandy beach below the headland.

He'd lost weight. They both had over past months, but tall and trimly proportioned he would still make heads turn when he walked past, His women patients who wished he had a more important role in their lives than that of G.P. wouldn't be having any second thoughts regarding that.

There was no sign of Phoebe and she breathed a sigh of relief. The last thing they needed was an audience at their first meeting in months. She hadn't expected it to be like this.

She'd imagined him opening the door of the house they'd once shared and being able to tell in those first moments of meeting just how pleased or otherwise he was to see her standing there, but this was nothing like that. Lots of folk they knew were milling around them in the snow-covered square.

As their glances met she felt tension pulling at her nerve ends. But in a grim sort of way it was as if her distaste for the circumstances of their meeting was being diverted by the sound of a woman's voice asking anxiously from behind, 'What's the matter, Bradley?' to be followed by a terrified plea of 'Somebody help us, please!'

She swivelled round quickly and saw Bradley

Somerton, the elderly organist who performed at the village church on Sundays, being supported by his wife, who was the one crying for help. He was gasping for breath with face purple, eyes bulging, and was choking. His mouth was wide open and she could see that his tongue was swollen and blocking the airway.

'Go and fetch Dad!' she cried to the children, and as they sprinted off she asked the organist's wife what he'd been eating to cause such a situation. At the same time she took hold of him, pulled him upright, and from behind gave him the treatment for a choking fit, arms tightly locked at the top of the rib cage and a sudden strong compression. It often did the trick, but not this time. No food or anything else came shooting from his mouth.

'He's allergic to seafood!' his wife cried, 'but he didn't eat anything like that at the wedding reception, which is where we had our last meal.'

A shadow fell across them and Ethan was there. 'Help me to lay him flat, Francine,' he said urgently, 'and then find something to prop his feet on to raise them.' He turned to the man's horrified wife. 'Has he got the emergency syringe of adrenaline with him that he's supposed to carry at all times?'

'Jacket pocket!' she cried, and within seconds he was injecting the lifesaving medication into the limp figure lying in the snow.

'It's anaphylactic shock,' he told Francine grimly, 'and unless the injection relieves the constriction of the lungs and airways in the next few seconds, we're going to lose him. We've been along this road once before, but the attack wasn't as severe as this. I might have to go to the surgery to get further supplies of the adrenaline if he doesn't respond. It's fortunate that it's just across the way. Can you ring for an ambulance? Even if he comes round all right from the one injection, I don't want to take any risks.'

She'd been checking the man's pulse and heartbeat, which were pounding out of control, and nodded at the request, explaining as she did so, 'I didn't get the chance before. Thank God you were near *and* knew his case history. But this kind of thing comes on almost immediately after eating food that the person is allergic to, so what has he been eating that his wife doesn't know about?'

'Bradley didn't partner me in the dancing,' his wife explained weakly. 'So maybe he's been to the stall that's selling food and drinks over there.'

The two doctors were only half listening. Francine was making the phone call and Ethan was watching keenly as the choking began to slowly subside and the tongue began to go forward once more leaving the airways clearer.

He gave a sigh of relief. The whole incident had taken just a matter of minutes, seconds almost, but if he and Francine hadn't been there…

She was switching her phone off and placing a comforting arm around the shoulders of the organist's wife and he thought for a moment that it had been almost like how it used to be with the two of them caring for the folks in Bluebell Cove.

He was still doing that, but *she* wasn't, and as he noted thankfully that the stricken man's heartbeat and pulse had stabilised he wondered what had brought her back to the place where she'd once been happy and contented.

When the ambulance had left, the children had gone to seek out their friends and for Francine and Ethan the brief feeling of togetherness that the incident had created hung between them like a question mark.

She was pale and shaking after the urgency of the situation, the need to act fast because a life had been at stake, and he placed his arm around her shoulders, held her close for a second and said gently, 'What a homecoming for you, Francine. Do you think that you and I deserve top marks for effort now that Bradley will live to see another day? We were right back on line like we used to be, weren't we?'

'Yes, professionally maybe,' she agreed stiltedly as panic took hold at the thought of him describing her presence back in his life as a *homecoming,* 'Though I'm only here on a visit.'

'Why didn't you let me know you were coming?' he asked, his voice tightening with disappointment.

'It was on impulse, a last-minute thing. I felt I just had to be with the children at Christmas,' she said awkwardly, knowing that she'd not kept to the arrangements they'd agreed on regarding who Kirstie and Ben should be with and when. 'I've put my things in the spare room. I hope that's all right.'

'No, it isn't!' he gritted. 'Take the master bedroom. I'll sleep in the spare room. The house is still your home as far as I'm concerned. So shall we go there instead of making a spectacle of ourselves in front of what is left of the wedding party?'

'Jenna and Lucas saw you trying to keep out of sight for some reason best known only to yourself and said to tell you that you're invited to the evening reception, which starts in an hour at the Enderbys' farmhouse.'

Kirstie and Ben weren't far away and he went on to explain, 'Needless to say, the children and I are going as I was best man for Lucas, and Kirstie was Jenna's bridesmaid.'

He looked across at the children, who were engrossed in throwing snowballs, and said, 'Don't spoil their Christmas, Francine.'

She swallowed hard. Kirstie had been a bridesmaid and Ethan best man for his friend *and she hadn't been there, and now he was warning her not to spoil their Christmas. Was this what she'd come to? Was his opinion of her now as low as that?*

Yet she'd had to tell herself the same thing, not to let the huge well of misery inside her loose on those she loved.

As they walked towards the house she said, to try and placate him, 'I haven't stopped loving this place, you know, Ethan.'

'But not enough to live in it,' he commented dryly.

'I haven't crossed the Channel to have all my shortcomings pointed out.'

'No, you haven't. Forget I said that.'

He wasn't to know that now she'd got what she wanted and was living in the beautiful house near Paris that had been her home during her childhood and early teens, she felt as if the price she was paying to live there permanently was too high, and she'd get the feeling of choking and breathlessness that came with panic.

She hadn't stopped to think things through properly when in hurt and anger she'd asked for a divorce, and now that it was under way and she was installed there, she was floundering instead of rejoicing, feeling that Ethan would never forgive her for the way she'd cared only about her own needs.

'I don't want us to change bedrooms,' she told him when they arrived back at the house. 'I'll be fine in the spare room. I didn't come to cause any upheaval and in keeping with that will give the wedding reception a miss, I think. Something tells me I won't be flavour of the month amongst your friends and the surgery crowd. I left them in the lurch when I went chasing off to

France, didn't I, even though I was only a part-time G.P?'

'You've got to come, *Maman*,' Kirstie pleaded. 'There will be lots of nice things to eat and music and dancing.'

'I will stay with *Maman*,' Ben said quickly, as an escape from something he wasn't looking forward to presented itself.

Ethan shook his head. 'No, Ben. There will be plenty of time for you to be with your mother over Christmas. You have been invited and are going, just as you would have been if she was still in France.'

'I'll come,' Francine said hastily, and as Ben's expression brightened she thought it didn't matter how people felt about her as long as the children were content.

Kirstie was keeping the pink dress on. She obviously adored it. Ben had changed into jeans and a sweater, replacing the suit he'd worn for the wedding, and Ethan was still in his outfit as best man.

It remained for her to find something to wear,

Francine thought, which meant unpacking her cases or rummaging around to see what she'd left behind in the wardrobe when she'd departed all those months ago.

There was an evening dress there of pale turquoise silk that Ethan had always liked her in. Low cut with a hooped skirt, it fitted better than it had ever done because of the weight she'd lost, and at the same time emphasised the dark chestnut of her hair and her beautiful green eyes.

When she went downstairs to where the three of them were waiting for her Ethan said, 'Did you have to wear that, Francine? The dress belongs to another life.'

'Do you want me to take it off, then?' she asked, with the feeling that so far she hadn't done anything right.

'No, of course not, we need to be off. I'm still in my role as best man until the evening is over.'

As he drove them along snow-covered lanes beside hedgerows touched by winter's frosty fingers, to the big farmhouse where the afternoon reception had already taken place, Ethan was wondering what really lay behind Francine's sudden appearance.

They'd agreed that the children should come to him from the middle of December until after New Year, and now she was here beside him looking pale and drawn with dark shadows under her eyes.

If only things had been different between them he would be holding his petite French wife close and wanting to put right what was wrong, but those days were gone for ever. The split was hurting beyond telling, and for his own part he was living with the knowledge that if he'd been prepared to leave the practice the two of them would still be together.

But torn two ways, he'd felt he owed it to Barbara Balfour to keep to the present arrangement. She had placed her life's work in his capable hands. For as far back as anyone could remember she'd provided those who lived in Bluebell Cove with first-class medical care and was now a semi-invalid, barely able to walk and relying on him to carry on the good work.

He and Francine had met at university where they'd both been studying medicine. They'd fallen madly in love, had had a fairy-tale wedding in Paris, and for twelve years she'd seemed content living on the Devon coast in beautiful Bluebell Cove.

They'd joined the practice originally as newly qualified G.Ps and she'd taken time out to have the children, returning when they were older on a part-time arrangement.

He'd known that she'd been homesick sometimes and had understood, agreeing that they should spend holidays and weekends with her parents whenever possible, but homesickness had never been the big issue that it was now.

It had been losing them and their house becoming hers that had made Francine want to go back home to live at the very time when there was nothing to go back for, or so he'd thought, but he hadn't taken into account the property on the outskirts of Paris.

Heartbroken, it had been her only comfort when those who'd lived in it had been taken from her. In the end it had won the struggle for her affection and he'd thought despairingly that he must be the only man living whose marriage had been destroyed by a house. Not because of adultery, or incompatibility, but by an attractive detached dwelling near Paris.

The farmhouse had just come into sight in a blaze of light, and as Ethan pulled up on the drive Francine thought this was what Bluebell Cove was all about, friends and neighbours looking out for each other, a caring community in a coastal setting that had welcomed her into its midst as a young French bride all those years ago.

The wedding couple were just inside the hallway, waiting to greet their guests as they arrived, and when Jenna saw Francine she beamed across at her in welcoming warmth and exclaimed, 'Francine, how lovely to see you!'

From Jenna's new husband there was just a cool nod and she got the message. Lucas would have seen what she'd done to Ethan and crossed her off his 'people I like' list, and she was prepared to accept that on the premise that maybe he'd never been so homesick he couldn't think straight.

During the evening people came up and said how nice it was to see her there. No one asked any questions, but it was there in their manner, an awkwardness that came from curiosity unsatisfied and a desire to cause no embarrassment for the respected head of the village practice.

There was one person it didn't apply to, however—the woman who had done the job for many years previously that Ethan was doing now. 'So you've come back to us,' Barbara Balfour said unsmilingly when they came face to face, 'and not before time. I'm glad to see that you've found some sense.'

'I'm just visiting for Christmas, Dr. Balfour,' she told her politely. 'I live in Paris now.'

'I see!' was the cold reply. 'And you've taken the children with you. Ethan doesn't deserve any of it.'

He wasn't around at that moment. Her husband was dancing with his daughter. Only Ben was with her and his mind was on other things as he observed the banquet that would shortly be available to everyone.

'Jenna is a lovely bride. I'm sorry I missed the service this afternoon,' she said smoothly, as if she hadn't just been taken to task. 'And now if you'll excuse me...' Moving away, she hurried towards the cloakroom before the tears she was holding back began to fall.

When the dance was over Ethan and Kirstie went to where Ben was standing still transfixed by the food and his father asked, 'Where's your mother, Ben?'

'Er, I don't know,' he replied. 'She was talking to Dr Balfour and then she went.'

'Went where?'

'I don't know.'

It added up, Ethan thought grimly. Francine talking to sharp-tongued Barbara and then disappearing. She must have gone home.

'I won't be long,' he told them both. 'I'm going to find her.'

As he hurried out into the lamp-lit gardens his step faltered. She was standing beside an ornamental pool, looking down into it sombrely, and he sighed. Francine had been right, he thought. It would have been better if she hadn't come.

If he'd been there when Barbara had accosted her he wouldn't have allowed it, but he hadn't been and where everyone else had been pleasant enough, that wasn't her style.

'Do you want to go home?' he asked when he reached her side.

She shook her head, 'No, Ethan. I'm sure I deserved to hear what Barbara had to say. You told me not to spoil the children's Christmas and I won't. I just came out to get a breath of air, that's all. Let's go back inside.'

For the rest of the evening she was how she

used to be. Smiling and relaxed. Dancing with the children in turn and laughing when Ben said, 'I don't mind dancing with you, *Maman*, but I don't want to do it with soppy girls.'

'What about you and Kirstie dancing all the way to the headland?' she teased. 'You didn't mind that, did you?'

'No, not really, but Dad said I had to because he wanted to dance with Phoebe.'

'Oh, I see.' And she felt she did.

Phoebe Howard was a lovely, uncomplicated girl who, the story went, had been deserted by her partner when pregnant. It was understandable that she might be attracted to someone like Ethan, and that he should be attracted to her after what *she'd* done to him over the last few months.

Yet Phoebe wasn't there tonight and it wouldn't be because she hadn't been asked. Surgery staff would have been invited because the bride worked there and the district nurse would be included, but as Phoebe would still be on maternity leave and didn't live locally, maybe she didn't want to spend too much time away from the baby.

On the other hand, it could be that the young single mother had seen her when she'd danced back to the square with Ethan and had gone because she'd observed that his wife had turned up.

It was time to leave, the wedding couple were starting their honeymoon in the morning and Ethan was having a last word with Lucas before they left regarding him being in charge of his property while they were away.

On their return his friend would be bringing Jenna to The Old Chart House next door to theirs, which Lucas had bought and refurbished when he'd come to live in the village.

When Ethan joined them and the four of them went to where he'd parked the car there was silence amongst them. Kirstie and Ben were tired because it had been a long and exciting day. Ethan was contemplating the misery of spending the night with Francine in the spare room, and she was envying the wedding couple for the freshness and simplicity of *their* love.

Theirs had been like that for a long time, hadn't lost the magic, until Ethan had taken charge of the practice and been so keen to make a success of it that she'd thought a few times that she and the children came second, just as Jenna and her father had come second to it during Barbara Balbour's reign.

She'd been twenty-eight and Ethan thirty years old when they'd had a fairy-tale wedding in a church in Paris, and now the precious thing that they'd had was dying because neither of them would give way to the other.

The children were in bed and after making sure they were settled with no televisions being switched on or mobile phones being used, Francine came downstairs to find Ethan making coffee in the kitchen.

'Thanks,' she said awkwardly as he passed hers to her. 'I'll take mine upstairs if you don't mind.'

He shrugged. 'Suit yourself. I'll be going to bed myself soon. It's been a long day, but I want to get the turkey in the oven first so that it will be almost cooked by the time I get up.'

'Yes, of course,' she murmured, feeling like an outsider in her own home, though it wasn't her home, was it? She'd forfeited the right to call it that when she'd gone to live in France.

With her foot on the bottom step of the stairs he was about to remind her of that fact by calling, 'The clean sheets are where they always were, though not as immaculately laundered maybe.'

As she lay sleepless between the sheets that he'd described she heard voices and laughter outside the window. In the next moment the beautiful words of a well-known Christmas carol were being sung and tears threatened again.

It was as if the fates were reminding her of what she'd thrown away by bringing to her notice every aspect of the enchantment of Bluebell Cove at Christmas. So far there'd been the dancing through the village, a Christmas wedding and now the carol singers.

In the middle of the night she could smell the turkey cooking quite strongly and wondered if the oven setting was too high. On impulse she crept downstairs in her nightdress to check on it.

It was a mistake. When she opened the kitchen door Ethan was there, basting the turkey. She turned to make a swift exit but he'd seen her and asked, 'What's wrong?'

'Er, nothing,' she said hurriedly, 'I just thought that it might be cooking too quickly.'

'I see,' he said evenly. 'Well, you can sleep easy as I've just turned the heat down, so go back to bed, Francine. Remember you're visiting. I'm in charge.'

She turned and went back up the stairs with the message crystal clear that she had overstepped the mark by butting into their Christmas.

'I'm in the way, aren't I?' she said the next morning while the children were opening their presents. 'I'll go as soon as there is a flight. There should be some on Boxing Day.'

'I thought you came because you wanted to be with Kirstie and Ben over Christmas and New Year,' he said levelly. 'There is no rush as far as I'm concerned. Just don't get any ideas about taking over now that you're here. As I told you last night, I'm in charge. I've had to be whether I wanted to or not.'

As he watched the colour drain from her face he was ashamed for letting his hurt manifest itself so clearly. Whatever Francine did, he would never stop loving her. He'd been just as inflexible in what he saw as his priorities as she'd been in hers when their difference of opinions had started to take a stranglehold on their marriage, so at least he should be civil.

At that moment Ben came dashing in, carrying the sledge that had been one of his father's presents to him. 'It's great, Dad!' he said. 'Can I go and try it out?'

'Yes, take Kirstie with you?' he told him. 'She'll want to have a try.'

'Not now she won't. She's too excited by what *Maman* has brought for her.'

'And what might that be?' Ethan asked.

'Fancy boots and a necklace.' He turned to his mother, 'The telescope is great, *Maman*.'

'And so are both of you, my darlings,' she said softly as he went chasing off to try the sledge.

At that moment Kirstie appeared, still in her pyjamas and wearing the boots and necklace. They smiled at the vision she presented and it was almost like old times for a moment.

Francine had come down to breakfast in a robe and slippers, not wanting to miss the children opening their presents, and now, with the memory of having been made to feel surplus and in the way, she went back upstairs to get showered and changed.

It was a strange sort of day, alternating between happy moments with the children and long silences when Ethan and she were alone. She'd noted that the turkey was cooked to perfection and wished she'd not interfered the previous night, and in keeping with her general feeling of being in the way broke the silence between them at one point to ask, 'Have you invited anyone round for Christmas dinner?'

'Such as?' he asked with dark brows rising.

'Er, Phoebe and her baby perhaps?'

'Phoebe Howard. Why would I do that? She does have family to be with, you know.'

'She was your partner when everyone was dancing through the village.'

'So? I had to find someone, and as she's been to see me at the surgery with depression a few times I thought it might cheer her up if I asked her to join me.'

'Ah! That is what Ben must have meant when he said you made him dance with Kirstie because you wanted to partner Phoebe.'

She saw his jaw line tighten and when he spoke again his voice was even colder than it had been in the kitchen in the middle of the night. 'Do you honestly think I would consider replacing you after so short a time?' he said. 'I valued our marriage more than anything on earth—you were the one to cast it aside like an old shoe.'

'Surely you see there was more to it than that, Ethan,' she reminded him in a low voice. 'Our differences of opinion were too big to ignore, and now that I'm here will you please let me help with whatever has to be done instead of shutting me out.'

'All right.' he agreed sombrely. 'We're both of the opinion that we don't want to spoil the children's Christmas so maybe it is best that you do help out.'

'Thanks for that, and I'm sorry I jumped to the wrong conclusions about you and Phoebe. It was just that I thought you deserved someone special to fill the gap I've left and that she might be it.'

He didn't reply. If he had done he would have told her that the gap she referred to would never be filled...that he didn't want patronising. *He* knew what he deserved and it was her, back in his life where she belonged. But it was too late for that. The marriage would soon be over. The solicitor's letter amongst the Christmas mail had confirmed that the divorce proceedings were progressing satisfactorily.

When she came downstairs later she was holding a gift-wrapped parcel and offering it to him said, 'I didn't want to give you this earlier as I was concerned that the children's excitement might be spoiled if you refused to accept it.'

'But it's all right if I refuse it now, is it?' he enquired quizzically.

'I'd rather you didn't, but it's up to you,' she said, and went back upstairs with the feeling that she'd made things worse again.

Yet there was light in the darkness. Shortly afterwards he came up after her, wearing the cashmere sweater she'd bought for him in Paris and been doubtful she would ever see him in it, and announced, 'If you look in the top drawer of the dressing table in the master bedroom you'll find a belated birthday gift and something for Christmas that have been waiting for you to show up, so that you might receive them in a less impersonal way than in the mail.'

'And you can't be bothered to give them to me personally?' she asked as a lump came up in her throat.

'Why, Francine? Would you want me to?' he asked gravely, and thought he was punishing her again because even in the present circumstances to have her beside him in the flesh was bringing joy to his soul.

'Yes, so either that or leave them where they are,' she replied, and went to gaze out of the bedroom window.

When she turned she could hear him going back downstairs and when next she saw him he had his cook's apron over the sweater and was preparing to serve soup and a sandwich for lunch to appease their appetites until the main meal in the evening.

CHAPTER TWO

FRANCINE was whisking the cream to go on top of the dessert she'd made for the Christmas meal and keeping an eye on the vegetables at the same time when Ethan announced, 'I've invited my parents for New Years Day. They've always come before and I don't see any reason to alter the arrangement. When I made it I didn't know you would be here.'

'Fine by me,' she told him with a sinking feeling inside. 'It will be nice to see them.'

'Yes, my mother maybe, but as you already know, my dad is a man who doesn't mince words.'

'I'll go out for the day,' she offered hastily.

He was frowning, 'The children won't want that.'

'They won't even notice. They'll still be engrossed with what they've had for Christmas.'

'Nevertheless I don't see why you shouldn't be there. Mum and Dad might feel hurt if you can't be bothered to spend some time with them. After all, they are not to blame for this situation.'

'And I am?'

'We both are,' he said grimly, 'but it's past. We've made our beds and must lie on them. To get back to what I was saying, it would do you no harm to see them. You've known them long enough. If Dad gets out of hand about the divorce, I'll deal with him.'

He was asking her to be polite to his parents, Francine thought wretchedly, *polite* to the kind mother-in-law that she loved. Jean Lomax had only moved from northern England to the south when she'd married his father, but had known what homesickness was and had understood how much she'd wanted to live in Paris in the house that was the only thing she had left of her parents.

She'd been sympathetic and supportive, but she loved her son and had accepted that he had to support his family *and* keep to the promise he'd made when he'd taken over the practice. Like someone on the rack, Ethan had been pulled both ways and she knew that he had stood his ground with an aching heart,

Her father-in-law, more volatile than his wife, had been furious with the French daughter-in-law that he'd always adored, and made no bones about it. The thought of coming face to face with him again made a chill run down her spine, but she would cope somehow for Ethan's sake.

'All right, if that is what you want.' she replied, wishing herself miles away. With tears threatening, she told him thickly, 'I'm taking the children back to France the moment New Year is over. I should never have come. It was stupid of me to think it could be civil between us, and as I'm already here it will save you having to bring them back the following weekend.'

He'd been putting crackers on the table while she'd been busy at the stove and knowing she was close to tears was gripping the back of a chair to stop himself from going to her and taking her in his arms. What would it achieve if he did? It was all too late, he told himself as he'd already done countless times before.

Their marriage was on the slippery slope, had been for months because he'd made a commitment that he'd felt he was not in a position to back out of, and Francine, who was usually most understanding and logically minded, hadn't been prepared to back him up on it.

When the four of them were seated around the table for what Francine was expecting to be a travesty of a Christmas dinner, Ethan produced the gifts that he'd told her about earlier, and with Kirstie and Ben watching intently she unwrapped them slowly.

The belated birthday present was a book that she'd once said she would like and she thought how achingly different it was from the lingerie that he usually chose with care.

There was an unwritten, unspoken message in the gift he'd given her and she understood it all too well. It was the same with the Christmas present, an exquisite gold bracelet decorated by a jeweller with tiny shells that he'd gathered from the beach. It was another reminder of what she was missing, she thought, beautiful Bluebell Cove with its golden sands and breathtaking countryside—and him.

'Thank you Ethan,' she said in a low voice and when Kirstie insisted on her wearing the bracelet she slid it carefully on to her wrist.

That night, sleepless once more in the spare room, Francine's mind was going over the day just gone and the strange mixture of it. The children's pleasure had been the highlight, and the giving and accepting of gifts between Ethan and herself bizarre and hurtful when she thought of how it had once been. Yet she was still wearing the bracelet, couldn't bear to take it off.

New Year's Day was going to be strange too with the visit of Jean and Lawrence Lomax planned. At the beginning of the marriage break-up Ethan's father had told her angrily that a wife's place was with her husband and if this was where he earned his living it was where she should be prepared to stay.

The dread of meeting him again was still with her, but he was the last person she was going allow to tune into the state of panic-stricken indecision in which she was floundering.

In the meantime there was a week's grace before she had to face them. She was going to keep a low profile where Ethan was concerned, spending all her time with the children or on her own. The feeling of panic was still with her, the choking sensation every time she thought of the years ahead without him.

If she were to tell him that she'd changed her mind and was going to forget about the house in Paris, would it make any difference? she wondered. The scars on their relationship were not going to heal overnight, if ever.

When she discovered that the children had been invited to the home of one of their friends for Boxing Day she decided to spend the time they were absent walking along the coast road and stopping off for lunch somewhere.

As soon as they'd left she went to get ready and came down within minutes dressed in a warm jacket, jeans and her boots. Ethan was reading a medical journal in the sitting room when she appeared and asked, 'Where are you off to? There's still a lot of snow around after the heavy fall on Christmas Eve.'

'I'm going to walk along the coast road and will eat out at lunchtime.'

He nodded and went back to his reading. There had been a time when he would have been beside her, she thought, happy that they were spending some time alone together, but not now. He was probably feeling relieved that she was going to be out of his orbit for a while as her role in his life had changed from cherished wife to intruder.

Outside there was a cold wind that stung her cheeks and the snow that had been there on the day of her arrival in Bluebell Cove still lay thick and crisp beneath her feet. Down below she could see the beach and the cold blue expanse of the Atlantic surging in once more.

In past summers when Ethan had finished at the surgery they'd spent lots of time down there, with the children fishing in rock pools and playing in the sand, and all of them swimming when the sea wasn't too rough.

It was far too cold for that sort of thing now, but she hoped he would still take Ben and Kirstie down there when they came to stay with him in the spring. The beach and the sea were two of the delights of Bluebell Cove, as was the enchanting village surrounded by the rolling green fields of the Devonshire countryside.

If she were to put all that on to one side of the scales of life, and on the other side place living in a house she owned on the outskirts of one of the most famous cities in the world and the place where she'd spent her childhood, *but had sacrificed her life with Ethan because of it,* which way would they tip? she wondered.

The wind continued to bite. She pulled her jacket more closely around her. What was the point of thinking those sorts of thoughts? She'd made her choice and her life was a mess.

It was going dark in the cold winter afternoon and Ethan kept looking at the clock. Where was she? he wondered, the pale and drawn-looking stranger who not so long ago had been happy to live with him here, and now incredibly was back as a visitor, sleeping in the spare room instead of next to him in the double bed they'd shared.

But, he thought bleakly, he wasn't there to watch over her in Paris, so why get all steamed up because Francine was late from a walk that they'd done countless times before? Yet he couldn't help himself.

When their marriage had started to collapse she'd been immovable in her desire to live in France and in the end he'd given up on her and after being stunned by her request for a divorce had agreed.

But she was different now, he thought, lost and vulnerable, but not so much that she hadn't been quick to remind him when he'd seen her in the square on Christmas Eve and joy bells had rung in his heart that she was only over on a visit *to see the children.*

He was going to have to keep a tight hold on his emotions because she'd been the one who'd wanted to end it, not him, and the pain of knowing she didn't love him enough to stay with him was unbearable.

He'd gone upstairs to find the sheepskin coat that he wore in this kind of weather, having decided that make of it what she would he had to check that no harm had befallen her, when through the bedroom window he saw her coming up the drive and hung the coat back in the wardrobe.

She was blue with cold and he thought it could only have been a desire to get away from him that had driven her out into the wintry weather for so long. What a fiasco Christmas was turning out to be, both of them wary as warring armies with undercurrents all the time instead of straight talking.

When he went downstairs she was in the hall,

taking off her boots and jacket, and he said, 'Go and sit by the fire. I'll make you a hot drink.'

She was opening her mouth to refuse, he could tell. 'Just do as I say, Francine,' he said, and she obeyed meekly.

He left her slowly sipping a hot toddy and went into his study, deciding that she didn't have to worry about him crowding her. It was the last thing he had in mind. He'd been dreading spending Christmas without her and now that she was here he didn't know which was worse—having no communication at all or the stiff dialogue that was all they were left with.

Everything had always been clear and uncomplicated between them. They'd been in tune in every way, including fantastic sexual chemistry, until Francine had inherited the house in Paris and her overwhelming homesickness had shattered what they'd had.

The children had just been dropped off. Tired and happy, they were full of the day they'd spent with their friends. As they were about to go up to bed Ben said, '*Maman*, we want to stay here where all our friends are.'

'Yes,' Kirstie agreed. 'We like it in France, but we have no friends there.'

Ethan watched the colour drain from Francine's face and thought that the children were quite unaware that they'd just dealt their mother a body blow. How would she react?

She'd been warm and drowsy after the cold walk, curled up in a big chair in front of the fire, but what they'd said brought her wide awake. As she was about to speak he motioned for her be silent, and ushering the children towards the stairs told them gently, 'It's late. Let's talk about it in the morning. Your mother has been for a long walk and is tired.'

He went up with them and waited until they were settled, and all the time he was thinking that he should be rejoicing at what they'd said. Francine wouldn't take Ben and Kirstie back to France if they didn't want to go. She wouldn't see her children unhappy, but neither would she be able to exist without them if they weren't under her wing. They would visit her, of course, like they did him, but he would have the most control over the situation, their roles would be reversed.

'I'm getting what I deserve, aren't I?' she asked in a low voice when he went back downstairs. 'I put my own needs before those of you and the children and am going to pay the price.'

There was no triumph in him, just sadness as he said, 'You'll find that Ben and Kirstie will have forgotten all about what they said in the morning. It was because they were on a high after spending the day with their friends.'

'You must hate me, Ethan.'

'Why would I do that? I've never had to live in a foreign land like you did, so I can't pass judgement on that, but I've learned one thing and it is that no marriage is a rock. I thought that ours was and it proved to be on shifting sands. I won't ever get married again, Francine.' And with that announcement for her to mull over, he went to make them a late supper.

* * *

Ethan had been right, Francine thought the next morning as the four of them sat down to breakfast. There was no repeat of the comments of the night before and the children went off sledging on a snow-covered slope nearby the moment they'd finished eating, but as far as she was concerned the words had been said and she couldn't ignore them.

It was the first time she'd heard anything of that nature, which could mean that the novelty of living in France was wearing off, and if that was the case, what was she going to do? She was feeling guilty enough already for what she'd done to Ethan. She didn't want to spoil their lives too.

They knew that things were not good between their parents and that the separation was going to continue, but she and Ethan hadn't explained about the impending divorce as yet. They'd been more concerned with showing them how much they loved them. Yet the day would have to come and she thought achingly that if only he hadn't called her bluff when she'd taken them to live in

France with her and had followed them, instead of letting it happen.

He was seated across from her at the dining table, waiting for any comments she might have, and she didn't disappoint him.

'Are you upset that the children didn't pursue their request from last night?' she asked.

'Why? Should I be?' he asked abruptly. He got to his feet, 'I'm due back at the surgery this morning so I'll see you whenever.'

It was like any day after a public holiday at The Tides Practice he thought as the morning progressed, made up of the regulars and people who had succumbed to various ills over the Christmas period.

The two nurses were being kept fully occupied as their third member, Jenna, the bride of Christmas Eve, was on her honeymoon. Lucy Watson, the elder of the two, had been a nurse at the surgery all her working life, and young Maria, a trainee, was the eldest daughter of one of the lifeguards down on the beach.

Leo Fenchurch, the new addition to the practice, wasn't his usual bright and breezy self and Ethan wondered if it was because he had been partaking too much of the wine during the festive occasion, but that surmise proved to be far from right when the two doctors stopped for a quick bite at lunchtime.

It seemed that Leo's lack of joviality was connected with something more serious than too much celebrating. His mother, who lived alone, was gravely ill and after a phone call on Christmas morning he'd been to Manchester and back in the last two days to be with her and to sort out a programme of care.

'What's the problem?' Ethan asked.

'Emphysema,' was the reply. 'Mum is only in her early sixties, but she might as well be ninety the way it's restricting her life. I shall go each weekend to check on her and do what I can, but will make sure I'm back first thing every Monday,' he promised. 'I haven't been here very long and don't want to mess you about, Ethan.'

'Look, Leo,' Ethan said. 'Do what you have to do for your mother—we'll cope at this end. How does the saying go? Charity begins at home.'

As he went back to his consulting room to prepare for the afternoon surgery and to make a call to Hunters Hill Hospital for an urgent appointment for a patient, Ethan thought he was the wrong one to be quoting that particular pearl of wisdom. There hadn't been much 'charity' over recent months in *his* home. Plenty of aggravation, but no charity.

The children had returned ravenous after sledging all morning and as Francine made them a hot lunch she put to them the question that she'd been debating all the time they'd been absent. It was asking for problems if she was going to risk a repeat of their disturbing comments of the night before, she'd kept telling herself, but she had to know for certain if they were unhappy away from Bluebell Cove.

Ethan had been right in his assumption that they wouldn't mention it again.

60 CHRISTMAS IN BLUEBELL COVE

So far they hadn't, but she couldn't face living on a knife edge, waiting to see if they would say the same thing again at some future time, how *they* felt about what was going on in *their* lives, as both of them were aware that a permanent split between their parents might happen one day.

It hadn't been Kirstie and Ben who'd acted totally out of character because they'd been overcome by homesickness, she thought, and if it had been, it would have been this place they were pining for, not the Paris house.

Ben gave her a chance to introduce the subject by saying, 'Grandma and Grandad are coming on New Year's Day.'

'Yes, I know,' she told him, smiling across at her son, who had the same kind of dark thatch as his father and the bright blue gaze, while Kirstie had skipped a generation and inherited Francine's mother's fair colouring. 'They'll be longing to see you both, but we are going back to France the morning after New Year's Day. OK?'

There was silence and she hoped it was because they were both tucking in to the food she'd just put in front of them, but it was not to be.

'We don't want to go,' Kirstie said apologetically, almost as if she understood how much it was going to upset her, and Ben, with his head bent over his meal, mumbled his agreement.

'Supposing I said you had to come with me? That you couldn't please yourselves. What would you do then?'

There was no reply forthcoming and she went into the kitchen and stood gripping the edge of the worktop until her knuckles shone white. Kirstie came to stand beside her and said awkwardly, 'We could still go to Paris for our holidays, Mum.' To Ben, who had sidled in behind her, she added, 'We would like that, wouldn't we, Ben?'

He nodded. 'Yes, as long as Dad is there too.'

'So it's all right if I go back without you, is it?' Francine asked, and was rewarded by consternation on both their parts.

'No! We want you to stay with us. Don't go back to Paris,' Ben begged.

'Why didn't you tell me before that you weren't happy there?'

'Well, we were at first. It was exciting, different, it was like being on holiday, but Bluebell Cove is where we want to live.'

Francine thought wretchedly that to a lesser degree than her own the children she adored had been made to feel homesick to satisfy her own longing. There was no way she could continue to inflict that on them, so what was the answer?

Go back to France alone? She couldn't bear the thought of it. But if she didn't do that, it would be a case of returning to Bluebell Cove defeated by her own shortsightedness, and Ethan wasn't going to welcome her back with open arms, was he? She'd felt like an intruder from the moment of arriving.

Two pairs of eyes were watching her anxiously and she managed a smile.

'All right,' she said comfortingly. 'I'll think

about what you've said and see what I can do, but why didn't you tell me this before?'

Ben didn't reply, he just stood looking down at the floor, but Kirstie had an answer for her. 'Because you kept crying all the time, *Maman*, that's why.'

They were off sledging again once their stomachs were no longer empty, with a strict warning to be back before it was dark. The moment they'd gone Francine put on her outdoor clothes and went into the centre of the village with a heavy heart, passing the surgery on her way and wondering what Ethan was going to say when he knew that she'd coaxed the truth out of the children.

He would have to be pleased, it went without saying. Only *she* was devastated by what Kirstie and Ben had said.

When she went into the estate agent's the face behind the counter wasn't that of anyone she knew, for which she was thankful. The doctor's wife enquiring about rental property in Bluebell

Cove when from all accounts she'd moved to France would have caused raised eyebrows, though no doubt it would soon get around no matter who attended her behind the mullioned windows that looked out onto the busy main street.

'Do you have any properties for rent?' she asked a smartly dressed young assistant.

'If you'd asked that in summer, the answer would have been no,' she was told, 'but at this time of year we do have a few. Top of the list is thatched Thimble Cottage, detached, fully furnished, with three bedrooms, bathroom with shower, sitting room, dining room and kitchen. All beautifully set out to match the age of the property. It is centrally situated next to the church. Are you familiar with the village at all?'

'Yes,' she said flatly.

'Thimble Cottage is available for twelve months. I'm not sure about afterwards,' she was told. 'Would you like to view it? I can take you now if you like.'

'Yes, that would be fine,' she agreed. 'If I am interested, I would want to move in immediately.'

The young assistant nodded. 'That would be no problem. Shall we go? I'll lock up here for a while.'

Francine had seen Thimble Cottage many times over the years but had never been inside, and when she did her first thought was that the estate agent hadn't been wrong in the way she'd described it. It was a very attractive property and might go some way towards lifting the gloom that had descended on her after talking to the children.

'This will suit me perfectly,' she said. 'I'd like to rent it for the twelve months it is available, so can we go back to your office and get it sorted?'

When the children came up the drive they were smiling and rosy cheeked from their exertions, but when she opened the door to them the uncertainty was there again in their expressions and any doubts she might have had about what she was intending disappeared.

But it was not yet the moment to tell them. Ethan had to be told first and though she was expecting him to be pleased that she'd had to give up some of her original ideas, she wasn't sure if he would be happy to have her back in the village, complicating their lives even more by living across the way from him.

When he came in it was half past six and she asked, 'How was your day?'

'Long and busy,' he said evenly, and went upstairs to change.

The children had already eaten. They'd been too hungry to wait and so it was just the two of them sitting down to the food she'd cooked.

When the meal was over and he was relaxing by the fire, she said tentatively, 'I've got something to tell you.'

'I hope it isn't that you're planning to take the children back to France before New Year,' he said immediately, 'because I won't allow it.

Mum and Dad will be bitterly disappointed if they're not here when they arrive.'

'Do you honestly think I would do that, knowing that they are coming?' she choked out.

His expression was bleak. Returning from a busy day at the surgery and finding her there would have been wonderful if the circumstances had been different. As it was, it had been bittersweet and he told her levelly, 'I didn't *honestly think* that you would ask for a divorce, Francine, but you did, so don't blame me for being concerned about what you might spring on me next.'

'What I have to tell you is the exact opposite to what you were thinking,' she said in a low voice. 'I'm not taking them back to France at all, except maybe for the occasional holiday. Are you pleased?'

He was observing her in jaw-dropping amazement.

'I might be if I knew why you've come to that decision, and then again, I might not. So what is going on, Francine? Is it because of what they said last night? Have they been on about it again?'

She shook her head, 'No, not exactly. I asked them outright if it was true and they said it was. They want to stay here—and want me to stay here too.'

'I see,' he said slowly, 'and what did you say to that?'

'I didn't *say* anything. Instead, I went out and *did* something. I've rented Thimble Cottage for twelve months and am going to live there with the children during the week, which is your busiest time, and will fly to Paris every weekend when they can stay with you. That way we will all be happy. Kirstie and Ben will be where they want to be, you will see a lot more of them. And I—'

'You will be sacrificing your dream for their sakes and mine.'

'I'll still have some of it if I go to France every weekend.'

'You could have done that in the first place Francine.'

Ignoring the comment, she begged, 'Just tell me that what I've done is all right.'

'Yes, I suppose so, except for one thing. Why rent the cottage? What is wrong with living here during the week before you go jetting off to Paris?'

She shook her head. 'It will be easier for us all, doing what I suggest.' She glanced towards the sitting room where Kirstie and Ben were watching television. 'So shall we tell the children and put their minds at rest? They were both reluctant to repeat what they said last night, but wanted me to know that it *was* how they felt.'

'Yes, all right,' he agreed, 'just as long as you are sure you want to do this.'

'It was the only solution I could think of.'

'Mmm. I suppose so,' he said dryly, and thought there was another one that she obviously wasn't going to consider. She could come back to him and tell him that it had all been a mistake.

But he knew that wasn't how she felt and he wasn't sure how he felt either. She'd been his love, the light of his life, and he'd lost her. Not to another man, but to a country and a house.

The children were slow to show their delight at the new arrangements until Francine held them close and told them that she was looking forward to living in Thimble Cottage, but would be going to Paris every weekend.

'So, you see, the three of us will live in the cottage during the week, and when I'm away at the weekends you will stay here with Dad,' she explained. Ben gave a whoop of delight, but Kirstie's expression was still anxious.

'We *did* like living in France, *Maman*,' she said guiltily. 'It was just as nice as here. What we *didn't* like was Dad not being there with us, and you not with us when we're here in Bluebell Cove. That's what was wrong.' A smile broke through. 'But what you've arranged will be super because we'll be near you both, and when you go over there at weekends we'll know that it isn't for long. So when can we go to see the cottage?'

'In the morning,' Francine told her, 'and I

think it will be fun for all of us, don't you?' she asked, turning to Ethan who had remained silent during her chat with the children.

'Yes, hopefully,' he replied as if 'fun' was a word that had disappeared from his vocabulary.

When they'd left them they could hear Kirstie and Ben talking about the cottage non-stop and Ethan wished that he and Francine could discuss things in their lives with as much enthusiasm, but it was as if they'd lost the art of conversation.

She'd given up her dream for them, he was thinking bleakly, the dream that she'd risked everything for, and he wanted to hold her close and comfort her in her moment of generous about-face.

He wondered sometimes if she realised how much she'd hurt him, but it wasn't the moment for that sort of thought as the children's happiness was washing off onto him and Francine was smiling as if she hadn't given anything up at all. Was it too much to hope that was how she really felt?

'When are you intending moving into Thimble Cottage?' he asked.

'Some time during the next few days, but I think the children should stay here until your parents have been. I'll pop across to see them, of course, but won't get in the way now that I've somewhere to—er—'

'Escape to?'

She nodded. 'I've asked for that, I suppose. How about calling it a place where I can keep a low profile?'

'Not in Bluebell Cove,' he said with a dry laugh. 'There will be lots of folk going past to get a look at the doctor's French wife's new home once the bush telegraph gets going.'

'I'm sure I'm not so interesting.'

'You'd be surprised.'

'So *do* you approve of what I've arranged for us all?' she questioned again.

'Shall we say that it's better than what we've had for the past few months and leave it at that,' he suggested, and went upstairs to bed with the thought in mind that at least he wouldn't be lying awake at night knowing that Francine was in the spare room and having to fight the longing to go in there, pick her up in his arms, take her to the bed where she belonged and wipe out the long lonely months he'd existed without her by making love to her.

It was going to be a strange set-up that she'd been arranging while he'd been at the practice, but Kirstie and Ben seemed to welcome the novelty of living in Thimble Cottage, Francine was more relaxed, and as for himself at least she would be where he could see her, know that she was safe and well, which would do for now, but the future felt as if it was shrouded in mist.

CHAPTER THREE

FRANCINE had taken Kirstie and Ben to see the inside of one of the prettiest thatched properties in the village the next morning and they'd loved it, which was one worry off her mind.

The fact that it was just across from the home where they'd been brought up suited them fine. They didn't see their mother moving into it in the same light as Ethan did. To him it was a relief that Francine was going to spend most of each week in Bluebell Cove on the children's behalf, but he also felt it was farcical.

He was torn between hope and anger at the latest turn of events. Hope because he thought that maybe Francine was being forced to take a fresh look at her priorities, and anger because by taking the children to live virtually on their own doorstep, another move for them, she was going to cause more disruption in their lives.

Had she so little love left for him that she couldn't stay in the same house? That she'd had to find somewhere away from him to keep a low profile, as she'd described it, for the time she was going to be in Bluebell Cove before jetting off to her dream home in Paris every weekend?

She'd been devastated to learn that the children weren't happy there and had been quick to find a solution, but there had been no consideration for *him* in it, just *their* welfare and what was most convenient for *her*.

Aware of Ethan's feelings, she'd left moving in until the morning of New Year's Eve, and as he'd been on the point of leaving for the surgery on the last day of the old year she'd asked if he minded if she took some sheets and towels with her.

'For goodness' sake, Francine, you can take whatever you like, they belong to you as much as me,' he'd said, adding with dry irony, 'I'm sorry I won't be available to carry you over the threshold. If I don't see you again today, just a reminder that Mum and Dad are coming tomorrow and *they* haven't committed any crime as far as you are concerned.'

'I'll call round for a chat.' She'd promised without meeting his glance, 'and, Ethan, I'll make a casserole and a dessert for lunch if you like.'

He'd managed a smile. 'I would appreciate that. It will allow me more time with them. I feel that I don't get to see them often enough.'

She'd turned away, but not before he'd seen tears on her lashes, and he'd cursed himself for being a tactless fool. Francine would never again have any prime time with *her* parents. They'd been taken from her in the worst possible way.

He'd stepped forward, wanting to hold her close and wipe away her tears, but she'd moved out of his reach and said flatly, 'You didn't understand then and you still don't. I can tell by the way you look at me, Ethan,' and leaving him to start his day with those comments ringing in his ears she'd gone upstairs to continue her preparations for the move across the way.

In spite of how she was feeling, Francine was smiling for the children's sake as they helped her move into the cottage. They thought it was going to be great having two homes where they could keep swapping from one to the other.

Ben and Kirstie would catch the school bus each morning as they'd always done while in Devon, and then on Friday nights would move in with Ethan for the weekend. Soon she would have to get in touch with the school where she'd enrolled them in France and explain the situation.

How Ethan was going to feel about the arrangement long term she didn't know, but ever since their separation 'long term' with regard to anything had ceased to have any meaning.

She'd asked for a divorce out of a need to clear the air, expecting him to flatly refuse. When he'd agreed without argument she'd been devastated.

So he really didn't care any more, she'd thought bleakly. Yet he'd been just as responsible as she was for the stalemate situation they'd found themselves in. Maybe he'd been looking for a loophole to give him his freedom and unknowingly she'd provided it.

From that moment on she'd put all the idyllic years they'd spent together out of her mind, and after that last rejection had concentrated on the divorce with just one thought in mind, the desire to bring back some life to the sad and empty house that had once been her home—

All her plans were falling apart, she reflected as she concentrated on the process of moving in. She'd just moved into one house and now she was moving into another because she couldn't bear to think of how wrong she'd been in taking the feelings of Kirstie and Ben for granted to such an extent.

While the children had been with her in Paris she'd been happy enough. They were her one remaining bond with Ethan, but being alone over Christmas had been more than she could bear and she'd put pride to one side and come back to the place she'd been so anxious to leave because without Ethan, Kirstie and Ben, the French house had been losing its appeal as a permanent home.

She'd told him that it was because of the children that she'd come over for Christmas, but she'd needed to be near him more than words could say, even though she'd known it wasn't going to be a 'merry' Christmas for ether of them.

During the rest of the day she moved the children's school clothes and their books into the cottage, ready for the start of the new term early in January, and made up the beds. Then went to do some food shopping on the main street of the village with top of her list what she'd promised Ethan she would make for lunch when his parents came the following day.

After tomorrow it would be time for her first weekend in Paris, which meant a flight to book, so after she'd been to the butcher's she went into the travel agent's next door and made a reservation for the first flight out on the Saturday morning, hoping that she would be leaving the children content and Ethan maybe mellowing a little.

She slept better that first night in Thimble Cottage. Maybe it was because she wasn't achingly aware of Ethan just a few feet away in the main bedroom of the house where she'd lived happily with him since they'd married.

Here there would be no awkwardness at mealtimes, or surging desires of the night as it had once been when the slightest caress would kindle the magical chemistry that had been one of the foundations of their marriage.

She would be near him in presence during the coming months, but far away in everything else, and if she hadn't discovered the children's true feelings about what might end up as living with each of them in turn once the divorce came through, she would have been far away from Ethan long term.

As matters stood now, with Kirstie and Ben living with her part of the time in the cottage and Ethan just across the way, she had the best of both worlds, or had she?

They were growing up fast. One day they would leave the two nests that their parents had provided for them and what of Ethan and her then? Maybe one day he would turn to Phoebe Howard, while she vegetated back in France.

It was New Year's Day and in the middle of the morning Francine saw the car pull up on the drive across the way announcing that Ethan's parents had arrived for what had always been a regular family get-together. After checking that the food she was preparing for lunch was cooking according to plan, she went across to greet them.

Jean Lomax was her usual delightful self without turning the meeting into a farce by wishing her a happy new year. Her mother-in-law would have grave doubts about the possibility of that for any of them, Francine considered.

Her down-to-earth husband's only comment was to the effect that he was expecting a cream tea. That he hadn't driven all the way from Bournemouth for something and nothing.

'Yes, we are having a cream tea, *Grandpère*,' Francine told him mildly, relieved that his mind was on food instead of *her sins* as he saw them, 'but first we are having lunch, which is going to be chicken casserole, and to tempt *Grandmère*'s northern palate, her favourite steamed suet pudding for dessert.'

'Sounds good,' he admitted. 'The right thing for a cold day.'

Ethan had just come in from checking that his father had enough petrol in the tank to get them home as Lawrence had been known to overlook such essentials on occasion, and he'd picked up the gist of the conversation.

He gave a half-smile as his glance met Francine's. The thought was there that if it hadn't been for the fact that the food was cooking across the way in Thimble Cottage instead of in their kitchen, he could almost believe that nothing had changed.

That it was another New Year's Day, another happy family gathering, but his frail-looking, yet never more beautiful French wife must be acutely aware that it was far from that. Unbelievably they were on the point of divorcing, and worse even than that, if anything could be, there were two faces missing and always would be because of a tragic mistake on someone else's part.

Kirstie and Ben appeared at that moment and created a diversion, having seen the car go past while they were sledging, and Francine asked them to lay the table once they'd got cleaned up while she went to check on the food.

As she got up to go Ethan said, 'I'll come across with you and help carry it when it's ready.'

'Are you sure?' she questioned.

'Of course I'm sure. What's the problem?'

'There isn't one. I just thought that—'

They were in the hall. She had her hand on the doorhandle, and turning she said in a low voice, 'I thought it might spoil your day, that's all.'

'It would have been more spoilt if you'd been in France,' he said levelly. 'At least in the cottage you're about as near as you can be without being where you really belong. But what about *your* day, Francine? You're with the children, which was what you wanted, but your parents aren't here and the pain of that must be beyond all telling.'

'It is,' she said still in the same quiet tone, 'but it is something I can't do anything about. I have to live with it.' And in that moment of truth the voice of reason spoke in the far reaches of her mind.

Yes, you do, it said, but you don't have to live with a failed marriage. You *can* do something about *that*, so why don't you climb down off your high horse and tell Ethan that you still love him? *Or is it perhaps that you don't, because he made you choose between here and there?*

She opened the door quickly and with him beside her crossed over the road.

As she was putting her key in the lock he scooped up a handful of untouched snow off the window sill and, cupping it in his hands, quickly made a snowball.

'Catch!' he cried, but she didn't turn fast enough and it landed on her shoulder.

All her hurts and worries were forgotten for a moment as she retaliated laughingly, then he threw another and in minutes they were having the snowball fight of their lives until, breathless, she pushed wide the door and ran inside to escape.

He followed and as they stood panting in the hallway like a couple of kids he said, 'If Kirstie and Ben have seen us out there, they will think we are out of our minds.'

'Mmm, but it was fun, wasn't it?' she replied, and as they observed each other it was there, out of the blue, the desire that could bring them into each other's arms in seconds. But the oven in the kitchen had other ideas about that and Francine cried, 'the food, Ethan, we came to check the food and the smell coming from out of there says that it needs to be removed from the heat without delay!'

He followed her into the kitchen and as she bent to take the casserole out of the oven he was close behind, so close he could have pressed his lips against the smooth skin at the back of her neck, but he knew that having just behaved as if they hadn't a care in the world it didn't give him the right to touch her, if only fleetingly. Francine was still his wife, but in namc only. The days were gone when after something like the playfight they had just had they would have gone upstairs, showered together, then made love.

Unaware of the direction that his thoughts were taking, she was checking that the food hadn't dried up. That the casserole was still moist and succulent and that the water in the steamer was still bubbling beneath the suet pudding.

She was already in trouble with her father-in-law and if lunch wasn't up to scratch she would plummet even lower in his esteem. But all was well and as Ethan quirked an enquiring eyebrow in her direction she said, 'It's fine, so let's go and feed your parents and the two young sledge fanatics.'

While she was covering the dishes with foil he'd been looking around the cottage that was going to be her temporary home and she asked warily, 'So what do you think, Ethan?'

'Seems OK,' was the less than enthusiastic reply and they carried the food across in silence, as if the fun and laughter they'd just shared had never happened.

Ethan's parents left in the early evening after partaking of the cream tea that Lawrence had demanded, and as the car disappeared from sight Francine gave a sigh of relief, and Ethan heard it.

'Surely it wasn't that bad?' he questioned. 'You stayed longer than I expected.'

'It wasn't,' she assured him, 'but I think your father let me off lightly compared to last time.'

'His bark is worse than his bite, you know that.

Don't take any notice. He's been discovering that what is happening is difficult to cope with, and who is to say that he isn't the only one.'

He was presenting an opportunity for them to talk about it, but she didn't take him up on it. Instead she told him, 'I've got an early flight in the morning and will see you some time on Monday. The new school term doesn't start until Wednesday so there's no panic for a couple of days.'

Early flight or not, Francine didn't sleep as well that second night in Thimble Cottage and when she got up to make a drink in the early hours she saw that the light was on in the master bedroom across the way.

So that made two of them, she thought and felt that the sooner she renewed her acquaintance with the French house the better. It might seem hollow and empty but that could be her fault. She hadn't done a thing to it since the day it had become hers, so maybe it was time she did. The task would help to occupy her mind with other things.

It had been an eventful Christmas and New Year, she thought as she huddled back beneath the bed covers, but apart from renting Thimble Cottage to please Kirstie and Ben, nothing else had changed in their lives. Ethan was still chained to the practice and showing no signs of throwing off the bonds that bound him.

He'd called round to see the Balfours over the holiday to tell Barbara about a practice manager who was starting in the first week of the new year and as always she'd been gratified to be included in what was happening at The Tides Practice.

Ethan always came back smiling when he'd been to the house on the headland because he'd made Barbara happy, and Francine didn't begrudge her that, but she sometimes felt that he mightn't feel so bound to the woman if he didn't see so much of her.

Barbara Balfour might be a role model in caring for the sick, but she fell far short when it came to family life, and Francine didn't want Ethan to fall into the same pattern because of his dedication to the practice. There had been an incident when he'd almost missed Ben's birthday treat, and that wasn't the only time he'd put work commitments above family ones. On that occasion, before they'd split up, she'd got tickets for the four of them for a show in town that Ben and Kirstie were eager to see, and was to be a birthday surprise for him. But at the last moment the quartet had become a trio because Ethan had gone out on a house call due to the transfer system to an out of hours emergency doctor not functioning.

It had been in a remote area out in the countryside and by the time he'd joined them the show had been almost over.

The birthday boy hadn't been concerned but she'd been upset and when she'd remonstrated with him he'd said, 'I'm sorry, Francine. There'd been a breakdown in the emergency arrangements and I couldn't ignore the call.'

'Correct me if I'm wrong,' she'd said angrily, 'but I seem to remember that there is another doctor in the practice besides you?'

She'd been referring to a young registrar who'd been working there at the time for experience in general practice.

'Yes, there is,' he'd agreed, 'but the elderly fellow I went out to was my patient and he's a cantankerous old guy at the best of times.'

'And was it serious?'

He'd sighed. 'No, not really. He had indigestion and was convinced it was his heart, but it just might have been and he was my responsibility because the emergency connection wasn't working.'

'I still think you could have asked our registrar friend. After all, it is Ben's birthday.'

'Yes, I know,' he'd agreed, and had pointed out that she appeared to be the only one upset by his absence and that it *was* his job that he'd been doing, caring for the sick.

Though his love for the three of them had been as strong as ever, she'd still had the feeling of 'them or us' and that had been coming from someone in the same profession.

* * *

There'd been the stillness of a community not yet up and about in Bluebell Cove as she'd driven through the village the next morning in the rented car that she'd been using, but it hadn't been surprising as it had been barely five a.m.

And now she was back where the other half of her heart belonged. Back in the quiet Paris house and not so sure that making it look more lived in was going to give her the pleasure she'd hoped for because she would have no one to share it with.

As the light began to fade in the winter afternoon she went into the city to shop for fresh food, and while she was there dined in a small restaurant that she was fond of to save having to cook when she got back.

The phone was ringing as she opened the door on her return and when she picked it up Kirstie's voice was there, asking if she was all right.

'Yes, of course, *ma cherie*,' she said quickly. 'The flight was on time and here I am. What is Ben doing?'

'He's here.' And her son's deeper tones replaced those of her daughter.

'You OK, *Maman*?' he asked awkwardly, and Francine thought it was a shame that the two of them should have this anxiety on her behalf.

'Yes, I'm fine, Ben.' she replied breezily. 'How about you?'

'We're all right except that it's been raining and all the snow has disappeared. So Dad took us to the cinema this afternoon and tonight we're going to a disco in the community centre.'

'What, your father too?' she exclaimed laughingly.

'No, Dad's dropping us off and picking us up afterwards.'

'Where is he now, Ben?'

'Here waiting to speak to you. Bye, Mum.'

'You arrived safely, it would seem,' Ethan said levelly.

'Yes, I'm fine,' she told him, keeping up the charade she'd presented for the children.

'So everything was all right at the house when you arrived?'

'Yes. I've just been into the city for supplies and had a meal while I was there, and am intending having an early night as I haven't been sleeping much lately.'

'Make sure that everywhere is securely locked when you go to bed,' he cautioned, while thinking that she wasn't the only one having restless nights.

'Yes, I'll do that,' she said mildly, and followed it up with, 'I've had to get used to remembering those kinds of things since I came here, Ethan.'

'Mmm, no doubt,' he agreed, 'and now I'm going to have to go as I'm driving Kirstie and Ben to the disco that they told you about. Then I'm joining Leo in the pub for a couple of hours, and before you ask, I will be *walking* the children home from the disco. If you remember, Bluebell Cove can be as beautiful on a cold winter night as on a warm summer one. There's frost shining like diamonds on all the trees and a full moon.'

'Yes. I'm sure it's lovely,' she agreed, 'but the

moon does shine over here, you know, and it *can* be frosty.' On that reminder she wished him goodbye and went to bed wondering if she would ever stop loving him enough to find happiness in the different way of life they were both contemplating.

After she'd hung up Ethan sat staring into space. After months of separation they'd been together for just one week and now she'd disappeared again, back to France, and instead of returning to him when the weekend was over she would be going to Thimble Cottage, snugly situated only yards away from what was her real home.

The children were waiting for him to drive them to the disco, hovering in the hall dressed to kill, and he held back a smile at the sight of Ben's hair covered in gel standing up in glossy spikes above his face.

He thought thankfully that his children were fortunate that they could walk away from what was happening in their parents' lives by going to things like the disco, meeting up with their friends, and would very soon be returning to school.

They weren't living on a tightrope like he was. Loving Francine and yet hating her for what she'd done to him, though, in honesty, could he blame her? Maybe his devotion to the practice *was* over the top, and it would be better if he wasn't so keen to carry the banner for Barbara's reputation all the time instead of just being himself.

He remembered discussing his failing marriage with Lucas one day and telling the man who was his closest friend how he just could not turn his back on the practice, that he owed it to Barbara to stand firm, and Lucas, who called a spade a spade, had said, 'Are you sure that it isn't because you think no one could do the job as well as you that you won't agree to what Francine is asking of you?'

'No! Of course not!' he'd exclaimed. 'When I make a promise I keep it, and that is what it's all about.'

At that time he'd been in no mood to dwell

on what Lucas had said. The fact remained that Francine had left him and taken the children with her, and he'd been appalled that she could do such a thing.

But now she had come back into his life and though it was only for the children's sake—he had no illusions about that—it was giving him food for thought, making him feel that somewhere there had to be a solution to the mess they'd made of everything.

'Dad, how long are you going to be?' Ben was asking as he surfaced from his thoughts. 'We've been ready for ages.'

He smiled at them both. 'Sorry, Ben. The hairstyle rendered me speechless when I saw it. Come on, let's go. Have a lovely time, both of you. Your mother will be thinking about you dancing away in the community centre and so will I. I'll pick you up at eleven o'clock on the dot.'

CHAPTER FOUR

SPRING had come to Bluebell Cove and the blue-bells that the village was named after were already gracing the borders of the hedgerows and carpeting the woods in bright blue perfection.

Francine was still living at Thimble Cottage and flying to Paris each weekend, leaving the children with Ethan, and he was holding the surgery together during Leo's frequent visits to Manchester to be with his sick mother.

She saw Ethan coming home quite late one Friday night and went across to ask if everything was all right at the practice. 'It's Leo,' he said. 'The guy has a lot on his mind. He has to keep going to Manchester, his mother is very sick. I did tell him when he first came not to worry if he had to be absent because of her ill health, that charity begins at home, but I can't keep on like this. I'm going to have to get some extra help.

'We're at full strength with three practice nurses now that Jenna is back on the job part time, but it's doctors we're short of. It was handy when Lucas was around as he helped out, but now that he's gone back to his consultant role at Hunter's Hill Hospital he's not available.'

'Why don't I come back part-time?' she suggested. 'The days are long once the children have gone to school, and during holidays I'm sure we can arrange some care for them at home with friends and so on.'

He was observing her thoughtfully. 'Are you sure about that? You moved into rented accommodation to get away from me and now you're suggesting an arrangement that would bring us closer together again.'

'Yes. I am sure. Do you want me mornings or afternoons?'

'Mornings are busiest.'

'Mornings it shall be, then. Is Leo away at the moment?'

'Yes, it could be for a while, and we're still short of another member of staff, though we do have a temporary district nurse. Phoebe's maternity leave won't be up until next New Year.'

'Where is she living? I haven't seen her anywhere around in the village since you danced with her on Christmas Eve.'

He was smiling. 'The reason for that is not because I stepped on her toes, I can assure you. It's because she's living with her sister in the town and rarely needs to come here for anything.'

'That will change, of course, when she comes back to work. What arrangements she will make for the baby when the time comes I don't know. But getting back to your offer of assisting at the practice, could you start on Monday?'

'Yes. I don't see why not.'

'Good. That will be great.' He was glancing towards the cottage and said, 'It all seems very quiet over there. Where are the children?'

'They're both involved with sleepovers. Kirstie is staying at the vicar's house. As you know, his daughter Jessica is one of her best friends. And

Ben is taking part in a twenty-four-hour fast for charity in the community centre with some of his friends.'

'I don't believe it!' he exclaimed laughingly. 'He won't last that long without food.'

'We'll have to see, won't we?' she replied, sharing his amusement.

His next comment took her by surprise. 'I suppose you're all geared up for an early night because you're off across the Channel again in the morning.'

'Not necessarily,' she replied. 'I've had my fill of early nights lately. Why do you ask?'

'Once I've changed into something more comfortable than this suit, I'm going to go for a stroll along the beach, and as you don't have to be here for Kirstie and Ben, do you fancy joining me?'

'Er, yes, I suppose I could,' she said hesitantly. 'Have you eaten yet?'

'Yes, I have. Maria went across to the bakery and got me some sandwiches before she went home.'

'Give me a buzz when you're ready, then,' she suggested, and went back into the cottage.

As she waited for him to ring, Francine knew that she was letting down another of her defences by offering to help out at the surgery, but she couldn't stand by and watch Ethan doing the work of two doctors and having the children at weekends as well. He wouldn't have a moment to spare, while she would be relaxing in France with all the time in the world at her disposal.

And now, without barely a second's thought, she'd agreed to go walking with him in the moonlight with the scent of bluebells all around them. She would have to keep a hold on her feelings and every time she felt she was weakening bring to mind the Paris house.

A little later, as they set off towards the headland and the beach below, she broke the silence that had fallen between them by asking, 'Why didn't Leo look for a position in general practice nearer Manchester if his mother is so ill?'

'Your guess is as good as mine,' he replied.

'I really don't know, but I'll tell you one thing, I don't want to lose him. He's settled in well with the patients, is a good doctor, and there would be no problem if it wasn't for his mother's health.'

As they clambered down the cliffside to where the beach lay smooth and golden between the tides, to Francine it felt like how it used to be. A special place with the Devon countryside around it dotted with fertile farms, hotels and guest houses amongst sweeping green fields, all of which had been part of the magic of Bluebell Cove before they'd separated. It was the place they'd come to as newly qualified doctors and she'd thought she would be happy to stay there for ever.

But she'd reckoned without circumstances, without the meddling fates. A new horizon had opened out in front of her, the opportunity to live in the gracious house where she'd been born.

It was a haunting moment, the two of them on the beach in the spring dusk.

Before the children had been born they'd once made love down there in the warm night when the place had been deserted. She wondered if Ethan remembered. He turned to face her and she knew by his expression that he did.

She stepped away from him, knowing she had to break into the moment that was wrapping itself around them. Any future life-shattering decisions she made would have to be in cold blood from now on, not in anger and frustration as before, or in the heat of the passion that could arise between them so quickly if they would let it.

So she said casually, 'Have you heard from your solicitor recently? Mine seems to be dragging her feet.'

Ethan had been content just to be with her, but not now, and his reply was in keeping with his expression. 'Why did you have to spoil this short time together, Francine?' he asked stonily. 'Yes, I've heard from my guy and he tells me that everything is going ahead as planned. Just think, you'll soon have what you've wanted, the freedom to live your life rattling around in that big house that was your parents'. Whoopee!'

'You know very well that isn't how I wanted it to be,' she said in a low voice. 'I wanted us all to live there, but it hasn't worked out like that. I had a dream, Ethan, and am sure you'll be pleased to know that it's fading.'

He was looking around him. 'I suggest we go. I've always loved it here down on the beach, but at this moment its appeal is missing.' She didn't move and he asked, 'Did you hear what I said? I'm not leaving you down here in the dark, so let's go, Francine.' As if she'd suddenly tuned in to what he was saying, she nodded and without speaking went before him up the cliffside.

When they stopped outside their respective residences he said, 'So, can I expect you at the surgery on Monday morning?'

'Did I say I would be there?'

'Yes.'

'Well, then, that is where I'll be. Goodnight, Ethan.' And without further comment she opened the door of Thimble Cottage and went in, wishing that she'd let their awareness of each down on the beach take its course.

The weekend that followed began like all those that had passed since that first one in January when she'd returned to France without the children. But this one was even more depressing because the frail truce between her and Ethan had been broken when she'd brought him down to earth on the beach on the Friday night.

As she unpacked her weekend case the desire to phone him and make amends was strong. But how could she possibly put things right between them when neither of them was willing to give up what *they* thought was right, and with divorce proceedings under way?

She was about to make the effort to food shop when the bell rang at the front door and she frowned. Visitors were not part of life here in Paris, she didn't know anyone that well, but it was ringing again, this time with an insistence to the sound, and she hurried downstairs.

When she opened the door her mouth was a round O of amazement.

Ethan and the children were standing in the porch, smiling at her expression.

'We thought we'd come to keep you company, didn't we, guys?' he said. 'So here we are. Aren't you going to ask us in?'

Was she going to ask them in? She was indeed, and throwing wide the door she said, 'You can rest assured of that! What a lovely surprise, Ethan.' She put her arms around her son and daughter. 'But why? You never said you were thinking of joining me here.'

'The idea only occurred to me last night, and as your flight was fully booked we came on the next one.' He was looking around him. 'I have to say I'd forgotten just how lovely Paris is in the spring, and what an attractive house this is.'

'Yes, it's lovely,' she agreed wistfully, 'but a house like this needs people to fill its rooms, to make it come alive, active people, happy people.'

'Do you mean to say that it's got the one but not the other?'

Glancing upwards to where Kirstie and Ben were dashing upstairs to their bedrooms, she said, 'It didn't have either until a few moments ago, but you've put that right for a short time, Ethan, so shall we forget our differences for a while and enjoy this lovely surprise that you've sprung on me? Does your coming here mean that you've forgiven me for the argument last night down on the beach?'

'There was nothing to forgive. You felt that we were asking for trouble, didn't you, that no matter how much we were drawn to each by the old magic, things are not right between us, that I needed a reminder, and I've taken it on board. So let's enjoy ourselves over the weekend, *if we can remember how*,' he said with a quirky smile. 'Which room do you want me in, Francine?'

'You'll have to share mine,' she said awkwardly. 'The children have the other two bedrooms. I use the big bedroom on the front, and the spare room is full of my father's business equipment. It has been sold and is waiting to be taken away, but the people have not yet been to collect it.'

He was observing her with raised brows. 'Are you sure?'

'What? That they are coming to collect it?'

'No. That you want me in your room.'

'It is twin bedded Ethan.'

'But of course,' he said with assumed gravity, and followed the children upstairs, leaving her to rejoice at the sudden turn of events. Dare she begin to hope that he was going to change his mind about them making their home here? she wondered. And if he did, would she ever forget the scent of bluebells and the pounding of the sea on to a golden beach in Devon?

The four of them spent the afternoon in the city centre, strolling around the shopping areas and art galleries. In the early evening Ethan announced that he'd made a reservation for a dinner cruise along the river Seine through the centre of Paris.

'How did you manage that?' she asked.

'I made it by phone after I'd booked the flight last night, and then it was just a matter of picking Kirstie up from the sleepover at the vicarage this morning and collecting a ravenously hungry Ben from the overnight fast at the community centre with a bag of sandwiches at the ready.'

It was magical, cruising along with a myriad lights illuminating famous landmarks and places of interest as they enjoyed the food. They'd done it a few times before but Francine thought it had never had more meaning than on this spring night with her husband. The husband who had refused to live in the beautiful city of her birth because of a promise to a demanding retired doctor.

But tonight they'd wiped the slate clean for a few hours. It was how they used to be, the four of them a happy family, and she hoped that somewhere in the ether her parents might be looking down on them and understanding how she was torn by her longing to be with her loved ones yet achingly homesick for Paris, even though today was the first time it had felt right being there.

The children were asleep, Ethan was watching sport on television, and Francine thought it was a good moment to end the day.

'I'll be up shortly,' he said casually as she began to climb the stairs, and she nodded without speaking. They'd had a lovely day, the four of them, but what was coming next was awful, sleeping in the same room in separate beds, and she intended to be asleep by the time he put in an appearance.

But sleep was hard to come by and when he appeared in the bedroom doorway dressed in a robe that he must have found in one of the wardrobes, she raised herself on the pillows and picked up a book off the bedside table.

He made no comment, just slipped off the robe and lay on top of the covers in his usual nightly attire, a pair of boxer shorts, but after she'd stared at the same page for at least twenty minutes he asked casually, 'Do you want a game of Scrabble as you're having trouble sleeping?'

When she looked across at him he was laughing, dark eyes warm and tender in the face that she knew as well as her own, and then he was on his feet and coming towards her and Francine knew if she didn't stop him now it would be too late, they would make love and the bliss of it would be wiped out by a feeling of bitter-sweetness because it could be the last time.

So why was she holding out her arms to him, throwing off the covers and letting him slip the straps of her nightdress off her shoulders? 'It's been so long, Francine,' he said as he caressed her from top to toe, 'we can't go on like this. I haven't stopped loving you for a second in spite of the arguments and misunderstandings, and pray that you feel the same about me.'

'Yes, I do,' she murmured as their arousal increased until she could think of nothing else but how she wanted him to bring her to the climax that she always achieved when they made love, and he did, until at last they lay content in each other's arms.

Ethan was the first to speak and she smiled when he said, 'I'm going to pull my bed across next to yours so that it's the equivalent of a double. I want you close through the night without us being cramped. OK?'

'Yes, OK,' she replied dreamily, with the delightful feeling that at last all was well with her world. Ethan had come to France for the weekend without persuasion and had enjoyed every moment he'd been there with her. Was the nightmare going to end and her parents' lovely home be filled with noise and laughter once more? She had a feeling that it was.

The flights for him and the children were for the Sunday night because it was school on Monday morning and he and Francine didn't want them to be no sooner home than having to go straight to school without time to eat and change into their uniforms, so on the off chance of flying back with them she rang the airport and managed to change her ticket.

She'd been up in the clouds all day after spending the night with Ethan and every time their glances met, her heartbeat quickened. The two of them had gone sightseeing in the morning, cruising on the river again afterwards, and had finally had afternoon tea in a small restaurant near the Eiffel Tower that served excellent food, before collecting Kirstie and Ben who'd spent the day with a group of the friends they'd met at their French school. And all the time Francine was rejoicing inwardly because Ethan was coming round to her way of thinking.

When he commented that the children were not supposed to know anyone on this side of the Channel, she just smiled and told him, 'Their reluctance to come here to live was mainly because you wouldn't be here. They can cope with living with me in Thimble Cottage because it is only yards away from where you are.'

* * *

There'd been no time for any really in-depth discussion after that with Kirstie and Ben around, so the bubble didn't burst until they were back in Bluebell Cove and the children were asleep. It was then that Francine went across to discuss the weekend's happenings with Ethan.

She found him on the phone to Leo and when he'd replaced the receiver he said soberly, 'No joy from that end. Leo could be absent for some time. You will be most welcome to join us at the surgery, Francine.'

'Er—yes, I suppose so,' she agreed doubtfully, 'but in the meantime you will have to make some arrangements for when we've gone.'

He was observing her warily. 'Gone where, Francine?'

'To Paris, of course. That is what was behind you coming to join me, wasn't it? The reason why we—' Her voice trailed away and there was a sinking feeling inside her as she said slowly. 'Did you make love to me just for the fun of it?'

'Of course not!' he exclaimed. 'I would never do that in a thousand years.'

'So why then? Not because you cared enough to make my dream come true obviously. It was just a one-off, was it?'

'No. It was not. When I came into the bedroom last night you were the most beautiful thing I'd ever seen, and no matter what, you were still mine. That was why, not for any other reason. To sleep with you wasn't why I'd followed you to France.'

'It was because I felt bad about the way we'd separated down on the beach and didn't want to have to wait until Monday before I saw you again. And with regard to me moving to France with you, how in the name of God can I? We've been through this a thousand times and it's not going to change, Francine. I can't do it.'

'You could if you tried.'

'Oh, yes? The practice in Bluebell Cove isn't clinical and impersonal like those in town centres. It's a place where friends meet friends, where they know their doctors, see them in the street and the pub, and are relaxed in their presence.

'When Barbara Balfour retired there was no problem in finding a replacement. They knew me almost as well as they'd known her, but it wouldn't be that simple if *I went*.

'Leo hasn't been here long. He hasn't enough experience of general practice to take over, *and* he's bogged down with family commitments. There is no one else who would be suitable. Our patients wouldn't take well to a stranger.

'Maybe sometime in the future a solution will present itself, but for now I just can't consider upping sticks and moving to France. I'm sorry, but that is how it is, Francine.'

'Fair enough,' she said flatly. 'So it's back to square one.'

'I'm afraid so—and what about tomorrow?'

'What about it? If you're referring to me working part time at the surgery again, we've already had that discussion, Ethan. What time do you want me there?'

'Eight o'clock, please.'

She was already turning to go and gave him a

cool nod of agreement. before returning to the cottage to weep out her disappointment.

There were a few raised eyebrows amongst the staff when Dr Lomax's chic French wife appeared the next morning with the news that she was about to join them in the capacity of part-time doctor.

When the man himself arrived looking somewhat frazzled after a sleepless night and having cut himself while shaving, she was already installed in the smallest of the consulting rooms after checking first that it wasn't in use by anyone else. And now, after clearing the desk of a bit of clutter, Francine was seated behind it, waiting for Ethan to arrive.

Of the three practice nurses Jenna was delighted to see her installed at the surgery once more. Lucy, who had been at The Tides Practice for years and was as fiercely loyal to Ethan as she'd been to his predecessor, had been polite but not gushing, and young Maria, the trainee, had flashed her a shy smile when Francine had found the staff gathered in the surgery kitchen, drinking tea, until half past eight arrived when the doors would be opened and morning surgery would commence.

The first thing Ethan did was to look around him for any signs of his wife, and Jenna said, 'Francine is already installed in the consulting room at the end of the passage, Ethan. What a nice surprise.'

'Yes, it is, Jenna,' he agreed. 'We are desperately short of doctors.' He smiled at Millie on Reception. 'It's just on half past you'd better open up, Millie.' And with only one thing in mind he strode briskly down the passage to the small room at the end.

'What kept you?' Francine asked from behind the desk when he was framed in the doorway. 'You aren't usually late.'

'True,' he replied, 'but having been awake most of the night, then dozing off just as I was due to get up—' he pointed to a gash on his chin '—plus doing this while I was shaving, it meant that I was on the last minute. Did you sleep all right after last night's misunderstanding?'

'Yes,' she said dryly. 'Like a top.'

It wasn't true, of course. She'd spent the night tossing and turning and the last thing she'd felt like doing in the spring dawn had been getting up to go and help at the surgery. But a promise was a promise and in spite of Ethan being around most of the time, it would help take her mind off the disillusion of the night before.

'So what do you want me to do?' she asked.

'How about forgive me for upsetting you?'

'I was referring to this place,' she told him levelly.

'Yes, of course you were,' he agreed flatly. 'I want us to share the morning surgery with you seeing as many patients as you feel possible. Obviously they will all have appointments with me as I've been the only doctor available of late, but I'm going to tell Millie to inform them when they arrive that they can see you if they wish and we'll play it from there.

'By having you to share the workload here, I'll

be able to start the house calls sooner and have a short break before afternoon surgery starts. At present there isn't a moment to spare between the two.

'It's going to be a bit chaotic at first as Millie won't be able to provide us with the patient's notes until she knows which of us they want to see, but hopefully it will gradually sort itself out.'

She nodded. 'It's quite a while since I was here the last time. Is there anything different I need to know, apart from the fact that this place is ruling our lives?'

It was said without animosity, just as a statement of fact, because after last night's discussion she'd finally given up the dream of them living in France. The cloud she'd been on since they'd made love had disappeared, leaving her in her usual state of limbo.

After observing the children's pleasure at being with their French friends again she was convinced that their comments about not liking it there had been more of a youthful ruse to get Ethan and herself as near to each other as possible, instead of a dislike of life in France, and that knowledge, along with what had happened between him and her, had given her the confidence to start hoping again, only to be brought back down to earth once they were back on English soil.

She'd decided as she'd sat unmoving for hours after leaving him the night before that she wasn't going to change anything with regard to Kirstie and Ben. They were settled back in the village, obviously felt secure regarding their home life, and liked the idea of Thimble Cottage. As for herself, she still had her lonely weekends in Paris to look forward to.

His reply to her comment about the practice ruling their lives had seemed to come from far away, so absorbed had she been in her own thoughts, but it registered just the same as Ethan said in a low voice. 'It isn't the time or the place to continue last night's discussion, Francine. Can I leave you to start your first day back in another part of Bluebell Cove where you are needed badly?'

'Yes, of course,' she said flatly. 'I'm ready and waiting.'

They were filtering through, mostly women patients, some of whom she knew from before, others were new.

Mary Carradine was someone she hadn't seen before and the smart elderly woman said on entering, 'I'm so pleased to have the chance to speak to a doctor of my own sex. I don't get embarrassed easily, I've been around too long for that, but I have got a little problem that I would rather discuss with you than a male doctor, basically because men don't have my kind of problem as they haven't got a cervix.'

'I had a hysteroscopy a few weeks ago and though the gynaecologist at the hospital said the tissue around the cervix was amazingly healthy for my age, when I got a copy of the report that he'd sent here it said that I'd got chronic cervicitis, which seemed odd after what he'd previously told me.'

'When I questioned it with the hospital I was informed that they would want to see me again in case they decided that a biopsy was needed with a view to cauterising the cervix. I'm due at the gynaecology clinic on Wednesday and felt I'd like to speak to someone here before I go.'

'I can understand your concern,' Francine told her. 'Our copy of the letter you received is in your file and I read it before I called you in, Mrs Carradine. First of all may I explain that of the two descriptions, acute and chronic, that might be used to describe your problem, chronic is the least serious.'

'In your case it means merely that the entrance to the cervix might need a gentle scrape. Maybe it requires a little tidying up. A scrape is more or less what it sounds like, it's a brief scraping movement to remove any infection in the easiest possible way. So try not to worry too much. Hunter's Hill Hospital has an excellent gynaecology department. You couldn't be in better hands. I shall look forward to hearing from you shortly that you are all sorted and seen to,' she said with a smile.

The patient got to her feet. 'I'll be glad when it's over,' she said wryly, 'but you've taken a lot of the worry from me now that I know what is involved. Thank you.' And off she went, a sprightly eighty-year-old who had been worrying about something she didn't understand.

After that Francine was kept busy for most of the morning, only stopping briefly when Jenna brought her a mug of coffee for elevenses. Ethan appeared just before midday and said, 'I've seen all my patients and am off on the home visits. There's just one person waiting to see you and then feel free to go. Thanks, Francine, having you here has made all the difference.'

As he went to his car on the practice forecourt he was thinking that it really had made all the difference, not only with the workload. Having her back in the building that she'd been absent from for so long was pure joy, or at least it would be if there was a chance that it would stay that way.

He wished he knew what the future held for them. Of one thing he *was* sure—he could not bear to lose her. Yet he doubted she felt the same way about him, especially after the way he'd allowed her to misunderstand his motive when he'd followed her to Paris and they'd slept together.

Sadly it hadn't been because he was ready to move to France. The opportunity to do that just wasn't going to present itself. He'd followed her there for the reason he'd given her, because of those moments on the beach on Friday night.

It had been like it used to be, the chemistry they'd created had been like an electric current moulding them into one. Because she'd felt it too, Francine had prevented what might have happened if they'd stayed down there with the comment about the divorce, and she couldn't have chosen a better dampener to put out the fire than that!

Yet he'd known that the spark was still there,

and all he'd been able to think about had been how much he wanted to be near her again to prove to himself that he hadn't imagined it.

What had happened when they'd shared a room had been proof positive that he hadn't, but he'd made a mess of it by giving her the impression he'd gone over to her way of thinking about living in France and it had turned sour.

Francine left the surgery at one o'clock. Ethan had phoned to say that he would be back shortly and for her to go whenever she wanted. Feeling the need of some time to herself away from her problems and those of others all morning at the surgery, she went across to the baker's and bought a sandwich and a cold drink, and in the sunshine of the spring afternoon decided to walk to the woods that lay behind the village for a quiet lunch.

As she was leaving the road to take the path that would lead her to them she didn't see Ethan's car approaching in the distance because she was too taken up with the bluebells all around her, but he'd caught a flash of white from the blouse she was wearing with a smart suit and pulled up on the grass verge at the entrance to the woods.

When she heard a twig break somewhere behind her she turned quickly, startled at the sound, and he called, 'Hi, Francine, it's me. I caught a glimpse of you as I was coming up the road. What are you doing here? It's a beautiful spot but a bit off the beaten track.'

'I wanted some peace, some quiet time, so I've brought my lunch with me,' she told him. 'It's such a beautiful day, too special to be inside when one doesn't have to be. Are *you* going to have time to eat?'

'Just about. I picked up a slice of fruit cake at one of the farm restaurants and a carton of soup. A lot of farms are going into catering these days, and very successfully too.'

She was moving towards the shade of an old oak tree that was a mass of fresh greenery and settling herself on a wooden bench nearby waited to see what he would do.

The memory of how they'd made love in the master bedroom of the house that he wouldn't agree to make his home was bitter-sweet. She would never come alive in any other man's arms as she did in his, but she'd been misled, hadn't she? Or maybe been too eager to believe what she'd wanted to believe.

It was an opportunity not to be missed, Ethan reflected. He had half an hour to spare before the afternoon surgery commenced so why not join her for lunch?

As if reading his mind, she said, 'Won't your soup be getting cold?'

He shook his head. 'It's in a special container that keeps it warm so I'm going to join you.' He felt her stiffen beside him and said reassuringly, 'To give you the chance to report on what you thought of the surgery this morning. I noticed that quite a few of our women patients drifted in your direction when they were told they had a choice.'

'It was good,' she told him as she munched on the sandwich. 'The time went very quickly for one thing, which it hasn't been doing of late, and being back on the job got the adrenaline going. Why don't you let me do some of the house calls when I've got settled in properly?'

He was smiling. The bright blue of his gaze warmed her cold heart, yet those same eyes had been wary and unapproachable the night before when they'd had yet another of their fruitless discussions about moving to France.

'Don't tempt me.' he said laughingly, quite unaware of the direction of her thoughts, and after that they ate in silence, as if the brief sharing of interest in the practice was all they had to talk about.

It was quiet in the woods, with only birdsong breaking the silence, and Francine wished she could stay there for ever, but Ethan was checking the time and saying he would have to get back, and when she would have stayed he said firmly, 'I'll drop you off at Thimble Cottage. It isn't a good idea to stay here on your own.'

She sighed. 'All right, but there is no one to fuss over me when I'm alone in Paris, is there?'

'I'm well aware of that, and now the children aren't with you when you're there I don't have a moment's peace of mind. Can't we keep the house just for holidays, and have you back here with us all the time? Surely you don't enjoy spending every weekend on your own in that empty place.'

'No, I don't enjoy it as a matter of fact,' she said soberly, 'but as I've already given up most of my dream by living here during the week for the children's sake, and now am helping you out at the surgery, which is a far cry from what I thought I would be doing when I inherited my parents' house, I am not going to deny myself the short time that I spend there.'

'Point taken,' he said flatly. 'And now, if you'll please get in the car, I'll drive you back.'

CHAPTER FIVE

As THE weeks went by and a golden summer took its course, life fell into a routine that Francine was grateful for in a strange sort of way, with the surgery in the mornings, swimming down in the cove in the afternoons, or driving out into the countryside for a cream tea, and always being back in time for Kirstie and Ben being dropped off from the school bus.

Concerned after watching Ethan arrive home late from the surgery night after night, she'd suggested that he dine with them to save him having to start cooking when he got in, and he hadn't needed to be asked twice as it created the family feeling that there was so little of between Francine and him in the bleak summer of their estrangement. The four of them sitting around the dining table, chatting about what the day had held for each of them, were times to be cherished.

There had been no further meetings like the one they'd had in the woods that day, or passionate nights that only led to further pain and uncertainty. They were both aware they had lawyers working in the background towards a divorce, and neither of them was on the point of changing their mind in spite of the fantastic chemistry between them that night in Paris.

After they'd eaten they would separate and wouldn't see each other until the next morning at the practice, and Ethan would console himself with the thought that at least they'd all been together for a short time.

Kirstie and Ben were on holiday in Austria with the school for the first two weeks of the long summer break and Thimble Cottage felt empty without their lively chatter and constant music in the background.

Ethan still came across each weekday evening to eat at her invitation, an invitation that she was having cause to regret as she was feeling low in body and spirit—body especially.

He'd asked her a couple of times if she was all right and concealing her listlessness she'd assured him that she was fine, but the moment he'd gone she'd been curled up on the sofa asleep.

It wasn't affecting her work at the surgery thankfully, but it occurred to her that it might have done if she'd been there to work a full day instead of just the morning. She put her lethargy down to her sadness and anxiety. It was so hard pretending to be indifferent to Ethan, watching him walk away from her every night when in reality all she wanted to do was give in to the temptation of curling up in his arms.

When Tom Appleby, the vicar's teenage son, was passed on to her one morning when Ethan had been called out on an emergency, she was at her most competent in dealing with a serious chest and lung infection that required an immediate X-ray and strong antibiotics to avert pneumonia.

His mother had been with him, anxious and

caring, intending to waste no time in taking her son to Hunter's Hill to be treated when Francine had explained what was needed.

When they'd gone she'd thought supposing it had been Ben in that state and she'd been far away across the Channel? All right, Ethan would have been there for him, but they were equally responsible for their children and living separate lives wasn't the ideal way of achieving that.

Her parents had always been there in togetherness for *her*, a united loving presence in her life. Would they want her to fall short of their example?

When Ethan returned from the callout she was in thoughtful mood but when she told him about young Tom Appleby, he put it down to that as she'd known him since he was a toddler.

It was on the day that Kirstie and Ben were due back from Austria that Francine faced up to the fact that she was pregnant. She'd begun to suspect she might be for a while. The signs had been lining up in front of her like soldiers on parade, a couple of missed periods, tiredness, tender breasts, and when nausea was absent, ravenous hunger, none of which could easily be described as symptoms of her underlying sadness over the state of her marriage!

They were all indications to a woman who had been pregnant before that she had conceived, and an early-morning urine sample had confirmed it.

When she'd discovered she was pregnant with Kirstie and Ben they had been moments of pure joy for Ethan and herself, but now it was going to be too complicated and upsetting for that kind of bliss. This precious child was going to be born into a shattered marriage because its mother had mistaken its father's intentions and in her aching need for his love had given in to it on a balmy spring night in Paris.

Today was Saturday and she was giving her trip to France a miss because she hadn't seen the children for two weeks. Ethan had suggested they all go out for a meal in the evening to celebrate their return and she'd agreed.

It would have been ungracious to refuse, but at the back of her mind would be the uncomfortable thought that she might start him thinking if she couldn't face the food. As a doctor he would soon pick up on any physical changes in her if she wasn't careful, and she didn't want the pregnancy brought out into the open until she had adjusted to the new development in her life.

She couldn't see there being any joyful celebrations this time and felt that if no one else in her family wanted to live in the Paris house with her, this new little one was going to, and Ethan was going to find out she'd fallen pregnant only when her condition was so obvious that she couldn't deny it.

Ben and Kirstie were home and talking non-stop about the holiday. Ethan had been to meet them at the airport and having them home safe and well and their mother staying in Bluebell

Cove for once over the weekend he would have been on top form if it hadn't been for observing Francine's listlessness when she thought no one was looking.

Surely she wasn't missing her weekend in France *so* much? he thought hollowly. She'd been delighted to have the children back and had a smile for him when he'd arrived with them, so what was the reason for the lethargy?

Yet she seemed happy enough in thc French restaurant out along the coast road where he'd booked the meal. The food was excellent and he hopcd it would go a little way towards her not having been home, as he was having to accept that Paris was now where she felt her home to be, and it took some swallowing.

But at least tonight they were together as a family again, he thought, and happy or sad, tearful or joyful, Francine was the most beautiful woman in the place with the dark chestnut of her hair falling in a shining swathe on her shoulders and those beautiful green eyes meeting his in a glance that was giving nothing away. Did she remember that night in Paris when he'd shared her room, he wondered, and they'd made love like there was no tomorrow?

He wasn't to know that she had every cause to remember it, remember it well. She was carrying his child, the child they'd created that night.

There were two more weeks to go of the summer break from school and the two younger members of the Lomax family were spending every moment on the beach or in the countryside while their parents were involved at the surgery.

Francine was still enjoying helping out in the mornings, but was hoping that Leo would soon be back as once Ethan knew about the baby she wasn't sure what would happen. At three months pregnant she was showing no signs of what lay ahead, but that was going to change in the near future.

In a few weeks time he would know beyond doubt they were going to have another child, if she managed to keep the fact to herself that long, and should have no difficulty in recollecting the occasion that had brought it about.

She'd had a weak moment one evening when Jenna and Lucas had called to see Ethan and she'd been there dropping off the laundry that she'd done for him. The newlyweds had announced joyfully that they were expecting their first child and when they'd gone she'd weakened and wanted to tell him that he was going to be a father again.

But he'd forestalled her by asking if she'd heard anything recently from her solicitor, and with the divorce they were involved in brought sharply back into focus it had proved to be a deterrent on his part, just as that time on the beach when she'd pulled the plug on a special moment.

The long light days of summer came and went with them eating together in the evenings and then Ethan leaving the three of them in Thimble Cottage to go back to his empty house, while at weekends Francine persisted in going back across the Channel to her own empty house.

It was a crazy set-up, Ethan considered as he took a solitary stroll into the countryside on one occasion after leaving the three of them doing their own thing back at the cottage. Yet Francine had met him more than halfway by finding somewhere to rent close by for the children's sake, and at least they were behaving in a civilised manner towards each other.

Whether she was happy about the situation or not, his beautiful French wife had lost the frailty that had been there when she'd arrived so unexpectedly on Christmas Eve, and seemed to have thrown off the lethargy that he'd been concerned about. As the weeks went by she was positively blooming in the clear air of Bluebell Cove.

Francine was a great help in the surgery. Even elderly Lucy, who'd been dubious about her returning to the practice under the present circumstances, had fallen under her spell, and the women patients were making good use of the presence of someone of their own sex to voice their concerns to.

Charlotte Templeton, plump, good-natured, and doing an excellent job as headmistress of the village school, was one of those who'd made an appointment to see Francinc about an infection of one of her nipples, and had been expecting to be told that a sore that wouldn't heal, and itching and burning in the area was eczema.

When Francine had explained that she was going to arrange for a biopsy to be done as it could be something cancerous the teacher, who never flapped on the job, had gone completely to pieces.

'There is a possibility that it could be Paget's disease of the nipple, a form of breast cancer that can easily be mistaken for eczema,' she'd told her. 'It starts in the milk ducts and if not treated quickly can spread further into the breast.'

'Oh, no!' Charlotte had cried frantically. 'I'm no good with illness. Never have been.' With a wail of fear she added, 'I don't want to lose my breast.'

'No one is saying that you will have to. This is just the first step,' Francine had told her consolingly. 'I will arrange an appointment for a biopsy to be taken at the hospital and from that we will get some answers.' The distressed woman nodded tearfully and she said, 'wipe away your tears, Charlotte. We cannot have those young ones who love their teacher so much seeing you weeping. The biopsy will be soon, and remember I may be mistaken, that it is eczema, but better to be sure, yes?'

'Yes, of course,' had been the reply, and with it had come an explanation for the distress. 'My mother died from breast cancer.'

'Not Paget's disease?'

'No. I hadn't heard of it until today, but it was breast cancer.'

'Don't let us be crossing our bridges too soon,' Francine had said gently. 'Let us see what the biopsy has to tell us.'

* * *

She'd told Ethan about the head teacher's problem that evening and he'd said, 'So is it likely to be eczema?'

'No, it is not,' she told him. 'I have seen it before. It is Paget's disease, how serious I do not know. I have told the hospital the test is urgent.'

'Hmm, bad news, then?'

'Yes, but we must hope it is not *too* bad. And how did your day go?'

This was like old times he thought, discussing what the day had brought for them at the practice, but not quite. 'Old times' had included peace and contentment in their lives and there was not much of that around at present.

'I had the results back on a fasting test that I requested for diabetes,' he told her. 'And they've come back positive. So Jack at the butcher's is going to have to keep an eye on his fats and sugars, which he won't like.'

'He wasn't keen on having to put his bacon and eggs on hold until he'd been to have blood taken first thing on an empty stomach, and the thought of having no sugar in his tea if it came back positive was taking on the mantle of a major catastrophe. I had to remind him that there are far worse things that some folk have to cope with than that.'

They were in the kitchen, tidying away after the evening meal as they'd been discussing the problems of their patients, and when they'd finished Ethan said, 'I'm meeting Jenna and Lucas in the pub for a chat later. Do you want to come along? Though I must warn you the main topic of conversation these days is childbirth and babies.'

'In that case, I think I'll give it a miss,' she said lightly. 'I might have a stroll along the tops or go down to the beach. It's too nice a night to be inside.'

'Fine,' he said levelly, taking on board the obvious fact that Francine was happy to tolerate his presence when Kirstie and Ben were around, or at the surgery where it was strictly impersonal, but when she had a choice she preferred him not to be around.

Where was it all going to end? he wondered. Not very happily from the looks of it, and how long was it going to be before some guy was attracted to a stunning French doctor who would soon be free from the shackles of her marriage, as that had to be the way *she* saw it?

How could she have endured talking about babies when she still hadn't told Ethan that she was carrying their child? Francine thought as she walked slowly down to the beach where holidaymakers and local people were enjoying the last hour of sunlight before it turned to dusk.

As she looked around her she considered that most of those frolicking on the sand and challenging the incoming tide with surfboards at the ready would think her insane in wanting to leave Bluebell Cove.

But the house in France was all she had left of loving parents and a happy childhood, and though Ethan understood that, his loyalty to his commitments here in the village came first and he did not want to leave them for a life across the Channel.

As she looked down at the beginning of a thickening waistline the evidence was there that another commitment, a joint one, was on its way, and she was going to have to tell him about it before someone else picked up on it first.

She began to retrace her steps with sudden urgency, hoping he hadn't already left to spend the evening with Jenna and Lucas. To her surprise, as she began to walk the short distance back to the village she saw him coming towards her, and she took a deep breath. Why not let this be the moment of truth? she thought.

Ethan would understand why she hadn't wanted to listen to Jenna's joyful mother-to-be talk when he knew.

'Why aren't you with Jenna and Lucas?' she asked uncomfortably.

'I was on my way and saw you in the distance.'

'Oh. I see.' Feeling as if her legs would give way beneath her, she sank down onto one of the wooden benches that were dotted along the cliff path and pointed to the space beside her but he didn't take the hint.

'We need to talk,' she told him as he stood looking down at her. 'Have you got a moment to spare?''

He almost groaned out loud at the question. Was it a reminder that she still felt herself to be low on his list of priorities?

'Yes, of course I have,' he said abruptly. 'What is it you have to say?'

'I'm pregnant, Ethan.'

'Wow!' he breathed collapsing into the vacant place beside her.

'Yes, and I'm sure you will have no difficulty in recalling how and when it came about.'

'None whatsoever,' he said huskily. His stunned acceptance of what she'd just told him had made his throat go dry. On a tide of rising joy he said what she'd been expecting him to say. 'And you've waited until you are almost four months pregnant before telling me? Yet I shouldn't have needed telling. Your listlessness and pallor during the first months and then a sudden blooming should have made me realise.

'I presume that you kept it from me because I'd misled you about the reason for me being in Paris that weekend. Because you still think I was only there for the sex.'

'You presume wrongly,' she protested. 'I didn't tell you because I was devastated at the thought of us bringing another child into a marriage that would soon be over. Obviously you would find out sooner or later, but I kept putting the moment off because I wasn't sure how you would react when you knew.

'I realised it wouldn't be long before you took a long hard look at me and tuned in to what was happening. No one else knows I'm pregnant. Even the children don't know. It would have been unforgivable to tell them before I'd told you.'

'I find it incredible that you had doubts about my reaction when I found out,' he said with his expression softening, 'and to set your mind at rest, here you have it.'

As she observed him warily he took her in his arms. 'I'm delighted,' he murmured with his lips against the soft chestnut hair, 'and I'm going to cancel the divorce proceedings first thing tomorrow.'

She shook her head. 'No. Don't do it for that reason, Ethan. It would have to be because we are both of the same mind about the future that we call it off, and we're not, are we? *I don't want this child to become a bargaining source between us. Do you understand?'*

'Only too well,' he replied flatly, 'but don't make any plans about taking the baby to live in Paris permanently, Francine. Two of us were involved in creating this new life, and two of us are going to be involved equally in its future, divorce or not.'

He was getting to his feet and looking down at her, sitting unmoving and white faced, said, 'I'll walk you home, it will be dark soon.' And without speaking she rose obediently and fell into step beside him.

No words passed between them as they walked the short distance to Thimble Cottage but their thought processes were working overtime and when they arrived he said, 'You weren't wrong when you said we have to talk and now is as good a time as any. Not here, though. We don't want Kirstie and Ben to find out they're going to have a new brother or sister from something they overhear in conversation. I'll phone Lucas to say I can't make it and if you come across in five minutes, we'll have the house to ourselves.'

'What have you done about antenatal care?' was his first question when they'd settled themselves on opposite sides of the sitting room.

'Hunter's Hill has me booked in for the birth and I've been attending the clinic there, which fortunately hasn't coincided with my working hours at the practice.'

'And is everything proceeding to plan?' he asked, feeling like a total outsider with regard to a momentous happening in his life

'Er, yes, so far, though there is one important matter we need to make a decision on, but not tonight Ethan, I'm tired.'

He didn't pursue that in the light of what she'd just said. Instead he referred to what they'd discussed earlier by asking, 'And you say the children don't yet know they're going to have a little brother or sister?'

'That is so,' she informed him, feeling that his questions were being fired at her like bullets from a gun. 'I want us to tell them together.' She managed a smile. 'At twelve coming on thirteen I expect Ben to be rather embarrassed, and at eleven Kirstie to want to be a second little mother to the baby, but we shall see, shall we not?'

'I don't know. Shall we?' he said flatly. 'It will depend on which of us is living where, I would think.' He glanced across to where the lights were on in the children's bedrooms. 'How about we tell them tomorrow? If we tell them tonight they'll be talking about it for hours, but it must be no later than that. I don't want them to find out from an outside source.'

'I know,' she agreed abjectly. 'I never seem to get anything right that concerns us these days.'

He couldn't let her think that about the child she was carrying, he thought achingly, and patting her cheek gently said, 'You can't describe giving me another child to love as getting it wrong, Francine. Go back and rest now and tomorrow we'll discuss our responsibilities to our surprise baby in more depth.'

She nodded and as exhaustion washed over her after the trauma of the last couple of hours she got to her feet, wished him goodnight and departed from the house she'd called home until the fates had presented her with an alternative residence—

They told Kirstie and Ben about the baby the following evening at the end of the meal and their daughter's eyes were round pools of delight as she cried, 'Really? Do you hear that, Ben? Mum is going to have a baby!'

He wasn't sharing her enthusiasm and asked, 'Are we going to have those nappy things all over the place and be woken up at night by its crying?'

As his parents exchanged amused glances Ethan told him laughingly, 'I'm afraid so. It will be just the same as when you and Kirstie were babies, except that you always cried the loudest.'

When they'd gone to meet their friends with instructions to be back before darkness fell Francine said on a more serious note, 'The implications of what we've told them haven't sunk in yet, but they will, and Kirstie will be the first wanting to know what the arrangements are going to be family-wise. In her own way she worries about what is going on between us.'

'The solution to that is in *your* hands,' he told her. 'You know my feelings. I certainly know yours, so it's stalemate. But it isn't fair to have Kirstie being insecure because of what is going on.'

'I'm renting Thimble Cottage as one means of preventing that, and no longer take the children with me when I go to Paris,' she reminded him.

'And you think that is enough?'

'I don't know!' she cried. 'Yet there is one thing that I do know.'

'And what might that be?'

'Your conscience doesn't seem to trouble you as much as mine does me.'

'So that is what you think, is it?' he said flatly. 'As every day goes by I'm seeing my dedication to the practice here in this beautiful place as a millstone around my neck instead of it being the satisfying and fulfilling job it used to be. The more we entangle ourselves in the mess we're making of our lives, the more I wonder if we ever loved each other as much as we like to think we did.'

'How can you say that?' she protested wretchedly. 'Surely you haven't forgotten that night in Paris?'

He didn't take her up on that. Instead he asked, 'So am I right in thinking that the discussion you mentioned last night was with regard to whether we go down the amniocentesis road and let them take some of the amniotic fluid to check for abnormalities or not?'

'Yes,' she replied gravely. 'In the past I've always sympathised with older pregnant mothers faced with that decision because of there being some slight risk to the baby in having the test. Now I'm one myself and at sixteen weeks into the pregnancy we need to decide.'

'And what did you usually advise those other women?' he asked with equal seriousness.

'That they take the test for their sake and that of the baby.'

He nodded. 'I've always said the same, Francine, so I suggest we make an appointment. I will be there with you, needless to say.'

He almost said that it would be helpful if it was in the afternoon as the morning surgery, which was the busiest, would be over, and if she could cope with the last hour of it on her own he could fit in what home visits had been asked for before noon.

But it was an occasion that put everything else into perspective and as if she'd read his mind Francine said, 'I'll ask for an afternoon appointment if possible as that would be less disruptive for the surgery.'

'It would be good if you could,' he said softly, 'but don't let them delay it because we have other commitments. The sooner the better for the test, Francine.'

They were going to have another child to love, he thought, and though he couldn't have it for her, he was going to be with her every step of the way, no matter what the future held for their marriage.

The appointment was made for the following Monday afternoon and the speed and the time of it were most acceptable. They held hands until her name was called to see the obstetrician and his staff, and as they presented themselves Francine knew just how much she needed Ethan there.

The ultrasound scan and withdrawing of the fluid didn't take long and when it was over they were told that the results would be through in a few days.

After she'd rested for a while they were ready to go, and as they were leaving Ethan said soberly, 'All we have to do now is wait and pray that the baby hasn't been harmed and the scan comes up clear.' Holding tightly to his arm, she managed a wan smile.

Their prayers were answered with a phone call to Thimble Cottage on the Friday afternoon to say that all was well. The baby was unharmed and the fluid had shown none of the danger signs they'd been testing for. As soon as she'd put the phone down Francine went round to the surgery to tell Ethan the good news.

He was on the point of seeing off a patient and when he saw her he observed her anxiously until she smiled, and then he was smiling too, and Millie on Reception was also beaming at the obvious happiness of the head of the practice and his wife.

On a Saturday in late September there was always a special event in Bluebell Cove where those who made their living from the land and the sea, or the turf and the surf as it was sometimes called, gathered to display the results of their labours and to compete for the honours bestowed on those whose efforts were judged to be the best.

It was held at Wheatlands Farm, the Enderbys' place, and like the Christmas ball they hosted every year for the people of Bluebell Cove, the show was always well attended.

This year would be no different. On a mellow autumn day they would come to compete for the top prizes in the different categories on display around the room.

George Enderby, the oldest member of the farming family, would judge the entries. Ethan had been nominated to chair the proceedings and Francine to present the prizes.

To complete the family foursome Kirstie would be helping in the café, which was always a great success, with George Enderby's daughter-in-law in charge, and Ben had been given the job of going round to check that the exhibits were not suffering from the warmth of the early autumn sun.

When Ethan and Francine had been asked to take part many months ago they had each expected that by the time the autumn show came round once more they would have either found a solution to the problem that was tearing them apart or would be divorced.

So far neither of those things had happened and they'd been wishing they weren't committed to being seen together in public on such an occasion, with the necessity of putting on a front for friends and acquaintances.

But as Ethan drove the four of them to Wheatlands Farm on the day the sheer pleasure of being together as a family on such an

occasion was wiping away regrets and embarrassment, especially for Francine when out of
the blue Kirstie said, 'Can we give our baby a
lovely French name like yours, *Maman*?'

Oh, you blessed child! Ethan thought as they
drove between high hedgerows that had been
bedecked with the glittering frost of winter the
last time they'd been to the Enderbys'.

Today the hedgerows were warm and colourful
with the last flowers of summer, and beside him
his wife was smiling at what her daughter had
said. His spirits were lifting. How could they
not, with such a thoughtful young peacemaker
in his family?

Kirstie was only eleven years old but pos-
sessed the wisdom and understanding of someone much older. As she matured she would be
just as attractive as her mother, but in a different
way as she'd inherited the golden colouring of
her maternal grandmother.

'And what names would you suggest?' Francine
was asking

'I don't care,' Ben said with his attention on the

sleek sports car in front of them, but Kirstie was quick to reply and again Ethan sent up thanks for his daughter.

It was with Francine's parents in mind that she said, 'How about Germaine, like *Grand-mère*, or Henri if it is a boy, like *Grand-père*?'

'I would like that,' Francine said softly, reaching over to the back seat to pat her daughter's cheek gently. Aware that Ethan hadn't spoken, she asked, 'As the baby's father, what do you have to say, Ethan?'

'I have to say it's a lovely thought and fine by me,' he replied, and thought did it matter where they lived as long as his family were happy?

They'd been coming with their entries all the day before, the long, the short and the tall, bringing flowers, fruit, vegetables, hams and bacon from the pig farms, cheeses from the dairy herds, and many other home-produced commodities. All of them prize specimens.

That had been yesterday. Today the fishermen would come with the best exhibits from their catch that morning, and those in charge of the show would be spending the morning arranging the entries in their various sections.

At two o'clock precisely Ethan would announce the proceedings open to those who had come from far and wide with their exhibits, and also to those who were there just to enjoy the spectacle of the fruits of land and sea. All of them entrenched in the community spirit that was always present on such occasions.

As he took his place on the podium Ethan thought there might be a few there who thought he had a charmed life. That he'd taken Barbara Balfour's place at the practice and was as well liked and respected as she had been, had a stunning French wife, two well-adjusted children, and lived in the big detached house across the way from the surgery that he'd had built by some artistic builder who had decorated the front of it so beautifully with pebbles from the beach.

If that *was* what they thought, they would be wrong. He did have all those blessings in his life and was humbly grateful for them. But the charmed life that people might think he had was a myth because his wife didn't want to live in Bluebell Cove any more and he was hurting every moment of the day.

Those who didn't know the circumstances might think him even more fortunate when they discovered he was about to become a father again and that it stood to reason his would be the bonniest baby in the village, just like the other two had been when they'd been small.

Yet as he looked at those assembled there he felt a moment of happiness. It might be short-lived, but Francine was beside him on the podium. Kirstie was down there with the rest of the kitchen staff, wearing a white apron over the pink bridesmaid's dress that came out on every occasion, and Ben was lounging nonchalantly nearby, holding a watering-can. With a smile and a few well-chosen words he opened the show and the proceedings commenced.

As he watched Francine presenting the awards with grace and style, giving no inkling of the pressures she was under, Ethan was aware of

Barbara Balfour in the front row of spectators and when all the awards had been given out and it was time for a traditional clotted-cream tea to be served, she called him across to where she was seated at a table with her family and said in her usual forthright manner, 'Did you know that we are going to be grandparents, Ethan?'

'Er, yes, so I've heard,' he said, grateful that Francine wasn't with him at that moment to hear the announcement. It would have been a reminder that *her* parents wouldn't be around for the birth of *their* new grandchild.

But Jenna was smiling her bubbly smile, Lucas had got to his feet and was taking a bow, and the moment passed in good humour with even his friend's mother-in-law managing a laugh.

He and Lucas had talked seriously about their respective wives' pregnancies one night when they'd gone for a walk along the cliff path together, and when Lucas had asked Ethan, 'How are things between the two of you?' he had sighed.

'I wish I knew,' he'd said. 'The future is

blurred. I can only cope with the present these days. Needless to say, we're both happy about the baby, but would be much more so if we had a clearer picture of each other's true feelings regarding the chaos our lives are in.'

'Francine does have a point, you know,' Lucas had said. 'One can't help having deep feelings about their childhood home, especially if it is in another country. I was grieved and angry on your part when she first went away, but she is doing her best now for you and the children, the way I see it.'

Ethan had groaned. 'Do you think I don't know that? If it wasn't for the practice I would do what she asks. But you worked there for a short time and saw what it's like. The people of Bluebell Cove feel blessed with the health care they receive.'

'And you still think no one can do it as well as you?'

'No. I've told you. I don't think that!' he'd cried. 'But a promise is a promise.'

'I know,' Lucas had agreed contritely. 'I only want you to get things in perspective.'

When they'd separated later Ethan had thought that wedding vows were promises too, some of the most important promises a person ever made, so what about those? But he wasn't the only one involved—did Francine ever consider that?

On Monday morning it seemed strange to Francine not to be touching down at the airport after the weekend in France and having to get to Bluebell Cove with all speed in time to have a quick bite before presenting herself at the surgery.

It was always a relief to know that on such occasions Ethan had seen to breakfast for the children and made sure they were in time for the school bus when they weren't on holiday.

She'd given Paris a miss because of the show on Saturday and was at the surgery bright and early to see her first patient, who happened to be Charlotte Templeton, the headmistress of the village school that she'd sent to have tests for suspected Paget's disease.

Francine had received a report from the hospital the previous Friday and was not surprised to see that she had booked an appointment to see her today.

When Charlotte came in she was pale but composed and as she seated herself opposite her first words were, 'I've had the tests that you asked for and have been given the results.

'They've told me that it is cancer but in its early stages. I'm going to have either chemo or radiotherapy, which should halt its progress and hopefully get rid of it, and am having my first treatment on Wednesday.

'That I can cope with, it was the thought of a mastectomy that threw me when I came to see you with the breast infection. I am deeply grateful that you picked up on it, Dr Lomax. My job at the school means everything to me and I don't want to let the children down.

'I'm rather like your husband, dedicated to the job. He gives his all to health care for the folks in Bluebell Cove, and I'm happily in charge of the education of our young ones.'

'From what they've said at the hospital I'm going to live to take another lesson, reassure another anxious parent, and at the worst pick up another piece of chalk, so that will do me for now.'

CHAPTER SIX

Autumn had arrived with its changing colours. The new school year had begun for Kirstie and Ben, and for the young ones in the village their headmistress was in control as always, with not a word to anyone regarding what was happening in her private life.

There were signs that Leo would soon be back where he wanted to be and where Ethan also wanted him to be. His sister was over from Canada, offering to relieve him of the burden of care by taking their mother back home with her to live.

In the very near future he would be taking up residence once more at the Mariners Moorings guest house on the coast road, where he'd stayed before.

'Do you want to finish at the surgery when we

have him back on board?' Ethan asked when he told Francine the good news.

'Not unless you want me to,' she replied. 'I'm enjoying being back on the job while I have the chance, and it won't be for long in any case. I will want to ease off by November as I'll be seven months pregnant by then and the baby is due in the new year so I will have to be making plans by that time.'

'*We* will have to make plans,' he said dryly, 'and I don't intend they should include you taking the baby to Paris with you every weekend when he or she arrives.'

What had started out as a harmonious discussion was beginning to fray around the edges.

'You've made your point,' she told him. 'At this moment I don't know what I want to do. The sensible thing would be forget about the house in France and take up where we left off when I inherited it, but I don't feel *sensible*, Ethan. I'm homesick and sad and want to wrap the only family I've got left around me like a warm blanket. Yet when I go there only emptiness awaits me.

'Because of the manner in which the house became mine it was all crystal clear where I wanted to be in the beginning. *I desperately wanted to live in France*, but that was before I'd heard what you thought of the idea, and in my mind there has been confusion ever since.

'For instance, my life now isn't very different from what it was before. I've already lost the battle because I'm here for the biggest part of each week to please the children, and am back in my old slot at the practice. I visualised a clean break with all of us moving across the Channel, but it hasn't worked out like that, has it?

'With regard to my moving into the cottage, I think I was manipulated a little by Kirstie and Ben on the matter of them not being happy in France. When the three of you surprised me by coming to join me that weekend, I noticed that they were off looking up their French friends the moment they arrived.

'It was as if they'd never been away, so I feel

it was more a case of them wanting us all to be together in the same place rather than not liking life over there.'

'So you are saying that nothing has changed much here,' he said levelly. 'Am I to take it that living in separate houses and no longer sleeping in the same bed doesn't warrant a mention, and that the feeling of treading on eggshells all the time should be ignored, when before we were like one being?

'If your parents had known this would happen when the house became yours, I'm sure they would have given it to charity. But getting back to what we were discussing, I would be most pleased for you to carry on at the surgery for as long as you feel up to it.

'Our women patients are most happy to be able to consult you, and the staff like having you around again. What is more, I might find time to do my own thing occasionally with both Leo and yourself to ease the load.'

They were in the garden at Thimble Cottage where he'd found her cutting the grass before the evening meal and had immediately taken over. Curious about what his 'own thing' might be, she asked, 'So what would you do if you had some free time?'

'Go to see Phoebe,' he said promptly. 'I feel bad that I haven't been more supportive towards her over past months since she had little Marcus. She is a member of my staff, even though she works on the district, and life hasn't been easy for her this past year.

'It would be simpler to keep in touch if she was living here in Bluebell Cove during her maternity leave, but she seems close to her sister who lives in the town and will have needed all the help she can get over past months.'

'So who is the father of her baby, do we know?'

'No. I haven't a clue. She doesn't seem to want to talk about it. Her leave will be up in the new year so that will be another valued member of staff returning. The only time she's been back here in public was when I asked her to be my partner on Christmas Eve when we all danced through the village.

'Phoebe wasn't sure she could make it at first, but when her sister offered to mind the baby she came, though she didn't waste any time when it was over. She was off like a shot.'

He was putting the mower away, unaware that Francine was thinking how thoughtful he was towards the young single mother, yet Ethan wouldn't move to France for *her* sake.

When he'd helped her clear away after the meal and the children were engrossed in their homework, he walked slowly back to the house in sombre mood.

Back there in the garden Francine had opened her heart to him more than she'd ever done since the split and deep down inside he knew they couldn't go on as they were. The situation had been complex enough before she'd fallen pregnant, but now—it really was like treading on eggshells.

Her surmise that Kirstie and Ben had pulled

some strings of their own to get their parents at least living in the same country was heart-breaking to say the least. How could he and Francine bring this kind of uncertainty into their youthful lives? There had to be a solution that suited them all and it was up to him to find it.

On her way to the surgery on the morning after their discussion in the garden Francine saw Mary Carradine doing an early shop at the butcher's. As they exchanged smiles the elderly villager said, 'They didn't do what I was expecting when I went to the hospital, Dr. Lomax. It seemed that I'd been worrying without cause. The gynaecologist said he was satisfied there was nothing seriously wrong with my cervix and I was discharged, which was wonderful news.'

Francine nodded and told her, 'He has informed me of his decision, Mrs Carradine, and I'm sure you must be relieved to know that is the end of it.'

'*I* am indeed!' she said with feeling, and trotted

into the butcher's with a lighter step than on the day when she'd been to the surgery to discuss her anxieties.

Leo was back, as bright and breezy as ever. Only a very close look at his fair countenance brought into focus the stress lines that caring for his sick mother had brought around eyes and jaw line.

Ethan told him what he needed was some good fresh air in his lungs, clear and unpolluted straight from the sea, along with some good Devon food, and the new addition to the practice said laughingly, 'Surely I don't look so bad?'

'No, of course you don't,' he said reassuringly, 'and even if you did, the food that Meredith serves at the guest house will soon put you right.'

'Yes, I'm sure it will,' he agreed, 'but what I really need to get me back on line is this chance to express to you my sincere thanks for keeping the place here open for me. It can't have been easy.'

'No, it wasn't,' Ethan told him, 'but Francine has helped out in the mornings and we managed. It's a shame that you missed the summer here in Bluebell Cove though. We're well into autumn now, but the place still holds many charms!'

In her small consulting room at the other end of the passage Francine was thinking along similar lines but with regard to herself rather than Leo Fenchurch.

When she'd been pregnant with Ben and Kirstie, nine months had seemed like for ever, but with this baby it felt as if the waiting time was going too fast because nothing was clear cut in her mind about the future. The days seemed to be rushing past at breakneck speed.

Soon she would have to do some baby shopping and now that Ethan wasn't so pressured workwise she knew he would want to go with her. Only that morning he'd said that from now on he was going to attend the antenatal clinic at the hospital with her, and the announcement had left her with mixed feelings of pleasure and uncertainty.

'So have you chosen some names for your baby, Dr. Lomax?' one of the antenatal nurses had asked the last time she was there.

The question had brought with it the memory of Kirstie suggesting they should call it after one of the parents that she'd lost so tragically and her young daughter's thoughtfulness and perception had been like balm to her aching heart.

She'd smiled. 'Yes, we have. Germaine for a girl, after my mother, and Henri for a boy, which was my father's name.'

'Those are lovely names,' the young nurse had said.

'Yes, they are,' she'd agreed softly, and wished that Ethan had been there to share the moment.

She was back in France again for the weekend and in the solitude of the house Francine was moving from one familiar room to the next deep in thought.

Would she have wanted to come back to live in Paris under different circumstances? If her parents hadn't died and the house hadn't become hers?

The truth was that she'd become obsessed with the idea of moving here, so much so that even the reality of her pregnancy hadn't really changed her mind.

She knew that the major part of her yearning to be back was because of the way her parents had been taken from her in a matter of minutes on a steep winding road in a foreign country. Coming to live in their house was the only way she could think of to ease the pain and at the same time celebrate their lives, but in the meantime what was she doing to her family? To Ethan?

Taking away the pleasure and satisfaction he got from the efficient running of the practice was one thing she was denying him, and another was depriving him of a proper home life.

He'd already announced that the baby wasn't going to be shuttled around to suit *their* requirements, and it would do Kirstie and Ben's education no good if they were involved in changing schools all the time.

She stopped in front of the wardrobes in the main bedroom of the house in her restless pacing. They were still full of her parents' clothes because she hadn't been able to face disposing of them. On a sudden impulse she began to take them out, placing the contents in neat piles on the big double bed.

Next she turned to the dressing table and started to empty the drawers with the same precision. Beneath an assortment of lingerie she found a long white envelope addressed to her in her mother's hand writing.

She stood looking down at it for a long moment and then opened it slowly. Her mother had written in a fine sloping hand.

To our dearest daughter,
We hope it may be long before you have need to read this, but when the time comes we want you to know that we will leave this

earth content because you have a husband who will always cherish you, two precious children, and are living in beautiful Bluebell Cove.

With eyes wide and astonished, fixed on the words in front of her, throat dry and legs wilting beneath her, she read the letter again, taking in the date at the top of the page. Her mother had written it the night before they'd left for the holiday in the Balkans, which was very strange, almost as if she'd had a premonition.

What about, though? That ill would befall them? That their daughter would need reassurance regarding her own life in the days to come?

She was shaking with the shock of finding what seemed like an answer to all her heart searching, and lifting the bed covers she crawled beneath them with the letter she'd found at the bottom of the drawer still clutched in her hand.

It hadn't been amongst all the legal papers

she'd had to deal with in the first instance after the accident. Instead it was as if her mother had been driven to write it and then with the holiday departure so near had put it out of sight.

At that moment the baby moved inside her, another reminder of where her responsibilities lay, and she thought that this unborn child must not be brought up between two homes, yet when she'd written the letter her mother would not have reckoned on her being totally overwhelmed by homesickness after losing them.

The weekends in Paris were never what she wanted them to be. They would be if Ethan and the children were with her, but as they weren't they seemed long and lonely and as a taxi dropped her off outside Thimble Cottage at half past five on Monday morning Francine was thinking that this last one had been in a class of its own with the sadness of finding her mother's letter and its contents creating even more confusion regarding the future.

As she put the key in the lock she ached to

have Ethan's arms around her and his voice telling her that it was going to be all right, even though she knew it wasn't.

She went upstairs and undressed slowly, intending to sleep before surgery to blot out the tangle of her thoughts, if only for a couple of hours. About to get under the covers, she looked across at the house where she'd once lived. The place where her husband and children were sleeping, and almost as if some unseen force was controlling her she reached for a robe, went back downstairs, and then like a fleeting shadow moved swiftly across the distance that separated the two houses.

She unlocked the door and then just as swiftly and silently went up the stairs, pausing for a moment to look in on the children in their respective rooms, and then opened the door of the master bedroom where Ethan was sleeping amongst tangled covers.

Sliding into the empty space beside him, she huddled into the curve of his back and as she did so he turned over drowsily, but was wide awake in seconds, observing her in amazement when he saw her.

Raising himself up on to his elbow, he looked down on her and asked urgently, 'What's wrong, Francine? Is it the baby?'

'No. I just came for comfort, Ethan, that's all. Not for any other reason.'

'So come here, then,' he said softly, cradling her to him, 'and tell me what it's all about.'

'I can't,' she whispered. 'I just want you to hold me.'

'All right,' he murmured, stroking her hair with gentle hands. As she moved closer he felt the baby move and sent up a prayer of thanks for the moment that had brought the three of them together, if only for a little while.

When it was time to rouse the children for school and get breakfast on the go, Francine was fast asleep. Warning them to be quiet, Ethan pointed to their mother in the bed where she belonged. As usual Ben had no comment to make but there was a big smile on his face, and Kirstie, once again the spokeswoman, said, 'Dad, is every-thing going to be all right again?'

'I don't know,' he told her. 'Your mother came because she was exhausted and distressed but wouldn't say why, so we need to keep our fin-gers crossed.'

Francine awoke to a room full of pale sunlight and the clock saying that it was half past ten. There was a note on the bed side table that said, 'You are to take the morning off, doctor's orders. Bacon and eggs in oven on low setting. Ethan.' As she sat on the edge of the bed, hold-ing it in her hand, the memory of another piece of paper came to mind and with it the thought that anyone reading her mother's letter would assume that she would take note of it. She *would* in normal circumstances, but normality was in short supply.

After she'd eaten she tidied everywhere gener-ally and collected all the washing that needed laundering, then went back to the cottage and spent what was left of the morning arranging for a charity shop not far from the house near Paris to collect all the clothes and other items that needed to be removed when she returned the following Saturday.

Ethan came in the lunch-hour and observed her keenly when she opened the door to him. 'Are you feeling better?' he asked as they went into the sitting room.

'Yes, thanks,' she replied awkwardly,

'So what was wrong?'

She couldn't lie, but neither did she want to tell him the truth. Not now anyway.

'I found a letter my mother had written to me in the event of their deaths just before the accident.'

He was frowning. 'That's strange. What was in it?'

'It was a farewell message to be read whenever the occasion arose.'

'So are you going to show it to me?'

'It was just the kind of letter that is left to comfort the bereaved,' she said, avoiding further truths.

'So?'

'I didn't bring it back with me.'

The frown was deepening. 'I can't believe you would leave something so precious behind in that empty house. Are we so far apart that you feel you can't show it to me, Francine?'

She shook her head determinedly. 'No, Ethan, we are not. It is because what is in it makes life even more complicated for me. I don't want to raise any false hopes.'

'Why, is Germaine telling you to stay where you belong, or something along those lines?'

'I'm not ready to discuss it yet.'

Sighing with frustration, he turned to leave. 'Fair enough. Hopefully I'll still be around when you are.'

'Why, where else are you likely to be?' she asked tightly.

He was smiling and she thought he deserved a medal for putting up with her whims and fancies, yet in truth they were more than that, much more. So why did no one understand?

'I might be with a rich widow on a cruise, or

go into a home for tired doctors,' he said whimsically, unable to be at odds with her for long. Anger and bitterness were long gone. They had been there in the early months of the break-up, but now it was a matter of being civil and trying not to hurt each other any more, which in some ways was a more depressing state of affairs because it was like giving up, waiting for the divorce to come through without trying to mend the wounds.

'I have to go. It's almost time for the late surgery. Don't bother with cooking tonight, Francine. I'll stop off for fish and chips at the Happy Fryer in the village when the surgery is over.' He was still smiling. 'The children will like that.'

'Yes, I'm sure they will,' she agreed with a watery smile of her own, and recalling the night before how he'd held her close and stroked her hair when she'd crept into bed beside him, she wondered how she could go on hurting him any more. Why not just give in and forget the dream? Even her mother was telling her to stay in Bluebell Cove. Not a single person understood how she felt.

Ethan was curious to know what was in the letter that Francine didn't want him to read, but not desperate. She would show it to him in her own good time and until then he would let it lie.

She was carrying their child and he wanted her to be stress-free as much as possible. But in the present state of their affairs stress was the name of the game and when they'd eaten the fish and chips that evening he said with a view to lightening up their lives, 'We've been invited to a cocktail party at the Enderbys' farm.'

'When?' she asked in surprise. 'And why?'

'Saturday night. It's to celebrate their daughter's engagement. So do you want to go? It will mean another weekend that you're away from your dream house.'

'Yes, of course I do,' she replied. 'Kirstie and Ben have got sleepovers arranged with their friends so the night is ours.' She would have to put her plans for the collection of her parents'

belongings by the charity shop on hold for another week, but for now she needed to mend
some bridges with her husband. It was time they
had some fun if there was ever any chance of
them having a future together.

I wish, he thought, thinking back to the days
when time together had not just been an occasional thing. Yet a tiny seed of hope had taken
root in his heart. It had appeared because she'd
come to him to be comforted, huddled in his
arms as if she'd lost the way and didn't know
what to do.

Obviously her mother had unknowingly said
something in the letter that had upset her daughter and it must have hit home, but next to the
seed of hope was a thorn. The thorn of Francine
rejecting his offer to cancel the divorce when
he'd discovered she was pregnant.

It was a mild evening for late October and when
they arrived at Wheatlands Farm there were lots
of folk there that they knew. Jenna and Lucas
were present, so happy that Francine envied

them again the uncomplicated nature of their love and hoped that nothing would ever come along to take the magic from it.

She and Ethan had been like that once upon a time, but she didn't want to think about it to-night. He'd told her she was the most beautiful woman in the room as he'd looked around him on arriving and she'd pulled a face and looked down at her spreading waistline.

'I mean it,' he'd said in a low voice as his glance had taken in the flowing black silk coat she was wearing over a low-cut cream dress. 'I've not seen the outfit before. Is it new?'

'Yes. Does it say Paris? It ought to.'

'You both say Paris,' he said in a low voice. 'I don't think anyone here would disagree with that. But the trouble is when they look at me they see Bluebell Cove.'

His tone was light but she shook her head. 'Don't let's start making comparisons, Ethan. Let's just be happy for once.'

Since reading her mother's letter calm was de-scending upon her gradually. There had been no great moment of decision, just a slowing down of the chaos of mind that she'd been living with for so long, and for the present she wanted to handle it with care. It was a frail and precious thing.

Their usual hospitable selves, the Enderbys had pulled out all the stops for their daughter's betrothal to a young vet. There was a DJ in charge of the music, a local band to entertain, and an abundance of delicious food.

While Ethan had gone to find them both something non-alcoholic to drink, Davina, the young bride-to-be, approached Francine and said shyly, 'I love your outfit, Dr Lomax, is it from Paris?'

'Yes, it is,' she replied with a smile for the girl that she'd treated for various things as she'd been growing up and who had always been interested in medical matters.

Her fiancé had appeared by her side and Davina introduced them. 'This is Rob, my fiancé, Dr. Lomax. He is going to be looking after sick animals, and I will be looking after sick people. I'm in my second year at medical school.'

Ethan was back with the drinks and he said, 'I remember your grandfather telling us that when you were young you were always taking his temperature and bandaging him up.'

'Yes, that's true,' Davina said laughingly. 'My poor dolls didn't have much of a life either, they were always ill beneath their blankets.'

Bringing the moment to a more topical level, he said, 'Our sincere congratulations to you both. May you have a long and happy life together, as Francine and I hope to have for ourselves.'

When Davina and Rob had moved on to chat to other guests Ethan said, 'I suppose that last sentence didn't go down too well with you.'

She didn't reply. Instead, taking his arm, she said, 'Let's dance, and if you hold me close enough you might feel this child of ours doing its own little dance. It is never still.'

'Hmm, so maybe we have a footballer, a rugby player, or even a sprinter.'

'Or it might be a little ballerina or a gymnast,' she reminded him.

'Of course,' he agreed, 'and that would be just as delightful.'

Barbara Balfour sat in her wheelchair at the edge of the dance floor, watching Ethan dance with Francine. She was alone. Her husband was chatting to a friend not far away and she had the moment to herself.

She would never admit it to anyone, but to her Ethan was the son she'd never had. Honourable, hard working, loving husband and father, extremely attractive, a man who stood out amongst his counterparts, and for months she'd observed his unhappiness and done nothing about it because she wanted him near her, not far away across the Channel.

Tonight he looked happy enough, she thought, but his wife blew hot and cold in the marriage. Maybe this was one of their better nights, but next weekend Francine would be off to France again, doing her own thing.

When she'd been so weak and ill the year before he'd called at their house every morning to check on her and Keith on his way to the surgery while in the background his marriage had been failing. Francine had taken the children off to France with her, leaving him alone in the big detached house that he'd had built for them.

At that time Jenna hadn't yet come back from abroad and it had been Ethan's visits that had helped her to get through the day. When their daughter had come home after becoming aware of her mother's ill health, Ethan had offered her a job in the practice that fitted in with looking after her.

She knew that the biggest part of Ethan's reluctance to do what Francine was asking of him came from the promise he'd made to her when he'd taken over from her that he would keep up the standard of care that she had always maintained, no matter what.

Little could he have expected that his dedication to his work would threaten his marriage and take him to the brink of divorce. *She* herself had sacrificed family life on the altar of healing the sick, and of late had thought if she'd had the chance to do it again she would have done it differently. So was she going to sit by and watch while Ethan did the same to a more serious degree?

Her train of thought was interrupted by Keith appearing at her side with food and drinks, and as she smiled at her long-suffering husband the moment passed, but would not be forgotten.

Unaware of the direction of Barbara's thoughts, Ethan and Francine passed by amongst the dancers and waved. She waved back and wished she still had the use of her legs so that he didn't have his promise to her clouding his judgement.

CHAPTER SEVEN

WHEN they arrived back at their separate residences on a high after a very enjoyable evening Ethan suggested, 'Why don't we spend the night together? You might recall that I do a very nice line in comforting.'

She smiled across at him in the shadowed light of the car. It would be easy to say yes to the suggestion, but she didn't want any more confusion with regard to her feelings. She was only just beginning to see the way ahead more clearly, and passion and the desire they aroused in each other could interfere with the process.

She shook her head. 'No, thanks just the same, Ethan.'

'So are we back to playing mind games again?' he asked disappointedly. 'You've been like you used to be all the time we were at the Enderbys', but once more in our own environment it's back to square one.'

'Don't be angry,' she pleaded. 'I've had a wonderful evening. Please don't spoil it, Ethan.'

'OK,' he said equably, and kissed her cheek fleetingly. 'I'll see you safely inside. I suppose tomorrow *is* another day. If I ever get used to this arrangement, you'll see a flag flying over the house we once lived in together.'

When she awoke the next morning Francine lay wide-eyed, looking up at the ceiling, and thought thankfully that the calm was still there. A sense of purpose hadn't presented itself so far but she knew it would come and when it did she would be ready.

The curtains were still drawn across the way and, remembering how Ethan had cooked her breakfast after she'd gone to him for comfort when she'd arrived home after reading her mother's letter, she dressed quickly and went across to where it seemed he was still sleeping.

Before she started making breakfast she took a

quick peep into the bedroom and, sure enough, he was asleep with the dark thatch of his hair stark against the whiteness of the pillow and his shoulders exposed above the covers.

It would be so easy to do a repeat of that other time and slide in beside him, she thought, but after the rebuff of the night before he might not want her presence so, resisting the enticing male magnetism of him, she went quietly back downstairs and into the kitchen.

The kettle was whistling and she was lifting the food she'd cooked out of the frying pan when she saw him framed in the kitchen doorway just as he'd rolled out of bed.

'What's this, then?' he asked drowsily. 'The calm before the storm, a sweetener before you tell me something I don't want to know?'

'No,' she told him steadily. 'It is in return for you making my breakfast the other day, that is all. So shall we eat?'

'Yes, by all means, when I've put some clothes on,' he replied, and disappeared.

The clothes he'd referred to turned out to be

just a pair of jeans and as they ate the food she'd prepared he said, 'This is nice. I can't remember when last we had breakfast together in this house.'

'It wasn't all that long ago,' she reminded him. 'There was the short time between my arriving unannounced on Christmas Eve and my moving into Thimble Cottage when we breakfasted together. Which reminds me, the rental period will be up in a couple of months.'

He was putting his knife and fork down slowly. 'And what do you intend to do?'

'Arrange to rent it for another six months. I spoke to the lettings person at the estate agent's a while back and she said it would be free, so it's just a matter of signing the agreement and paying the rental.'

'I can't believe it!' he said tightly. 'This farce seems to be going on for ever.' He was getting up from the table, pushing his chair back and heading upstairs again. Moments later she heard the shower in the en suite running and when he came down again he was dressed in smart clothes. She was impelled to ask, 'Where are you off to?'

'I'm going to do what I promised myself I would do when I had the time. Something I should have done before—check that Phoebe is all right.'

'Lucky Phoebe,' she said in a low voice.

'Well, *you* don't need me around here, do you? You've got everything nicely planned, with weekends in France, your own place just across the way, the children with you all the time on weekdays, while I get my slot just when it suits you.'

As he slammed the door behind him a picture fell off the wall and as she bent to pick it up the baby moved as if to remind her that her responsibilities didn't end there.

Like a lot of good-natured people who are rarely angry, when Ethan lost his temper there was no mistaking it. He had to be pushed beyond reason to be so angry, and she couldn't blame him.

He hadn't given her time to explain that she

wasn't expecting to be in Thimble Cottage for another six months, or even six weeks, but if she didn't rent it again she could be left with a situation where she might have to move back here before she was ready to do so.

There were bridges to mend *and cross*, legal matters to deal with, and the birth of their child drawing nearer all the time. The two of them were not going to slip back into an easy relationship so smoothly.

The church bells were pealing out over the sleeping village as she walked back to the cottage in the peaceful Sunday morning, and expecting that it would be around lunchtime before Kirstie and Ben surfaced she went inside for a jacket and set off for a walk along the coastal path.

It was chilly with a cold wind blowing in from the sea. Down below the tide was coming in, surging onto the sand with its own special kind of magnificence and putting into perspective all her uncertainties and yearnings with the infinity of the scene.

When she looked up Ben and Kirstie were coming towards her with eyelids drooping from lack of sleep and looking as if they'd slept in their clothes, but when they saw her they came running towards her, tiredness forgotten in the pleasure of meeting, even though they'd only been apart from her since the night before.

At the same time Ethan pulled up alongside on the road that ran beside the path and she thought, These are my family, my loved ones, and as long as I have them nothing else matters.

As the three of them piled into the car she said, 'You haven't been gone long. Did you manage to find Phoebe?'

'Yes. I only stayed a short time, though. She's all right and little Marcus is coming along fine. She confirmed that she'll be back in the new year and when she said she'll be looking for somewhere to rent in Bluebell Cove I offered her one of the apartments over the surgery. They're both vacant at the moment and it occurred to me that if he can tear himself away from Meredith's cooking, Leo might be interested in the other one.'

'And what did Phoebe say when you suggested it?'

'Accepted on the spot, so that is sorted.' He glanced at the sleepover pair in the back seat, 'As we're all together how about we go somewhere for Sunday lunch, or maybe Sunday brunch if you haven't had any breakfast?'

It seemed that Kirstie and Ben *hadn't* had any breakfast, so brunch it was beside a big log fire in a farmhouse out in the countryside that had a restaurant.

Francine said little during the meal. Instead she listened to Ethan and the children chattering about various things and kept her thoughts to herself. He observed her curiously from time to time yet made no comment, but when they were driving home he said in a low voice, 'Are you all right? You've hardly spoken since I picked you up on the coast road. Is it because of my bad temper at breakfast-time when I went storming off?'

She shook her head. 'No. I'm fine. I've just been relaxing, that's all.'

The time wasn't yet right to tell Ethan she was relinquishing the dream. She was expecting him to be delighted, but over-confidence never did anyone any good and neither did taking things for granted. Suppose when she told him he was dubious after all the aggravation she'd caused?

On Monday morning the weather took a turn for the worse, with driving rain and gale-force winds reminding the residents of Bluebell Cove that winter was stating its case and that November, one of the dreariest months of the year, would soon be upon them.

The month that was the forerunner to December and Christmas did have one redeeming feature, though. It brought with it Bonfire Night on the fifth, and already preparations for the event were under way on the headland,

Francine was due at the antenatal clinic at the hospital in the afternoon and once again

Ethan intended to be there when she saw the gynaecologist.

When he came to pick her up he said, 'The weather is worsening. I hope Kirstie and Ben have the sense not to hang about when the school bus drops them off, otherwise they'll be drenched.'

She had been given a clean bill of health regarding her pregnancy and when the gynaecologist had asked if they'd been told the sex of the baby they'd smiled at each other and shaken their heads.

'We don't want to know,' Ethan had told him. 'We will be delighted whatever it is, won't we, Francine?' And for a heavenly moment she'd felt as if they were just like any other expectant parents, with the safe arrival of their child the only thing to concern themselves about.

Living in separate houses with a divorce pending hardly put them in that category, but for a fraction of time she was going to forget that, push the downside of their lives to the back of her mind.

As they were leaving the clinic Ethan suggested they go for a coffee in the hospital restaurant and so, tranquil and relaxed, she agreed.

They were enjoying the drink in the middle of the winter afternoon with no feeling of urgency when an item of local news flashed onto a television screen close by and changed all that.

It said there had been an accident on a side road approaching Bluebell Cove. A school bus had been hit by a falling tree brought down by high winds coming in from the sea, and as they looked at each other aghast Ethan said, 'There are lots of buses on the roads at this time of day, Francine, so don't—'

His voice trailed away as further information was released to the effect that the quick thinking of one of the pupils on the bus, Ben Lomax, had averted what could have been a terrible disaster and he was hero of the hour.

The tree had smashed into the driving compartment and the driver had been knocked senseless, slumped over the wheel with the vehicle out of control and the young passengers being thrown all over the place, until Ben had rushed to the front and found the brakes.

The announcement went on to say that he had refused to be interviewed because his younger sister had been hurt and he wanted to be with her in the ambulance, and as if to add to the horror of the moment the two doctors heard the sirens of several ambulances screeching onto the forecourt outside A and E.

They were on their feet and running before the noise had stopped. The fact that Francine was almost seven months pregnant did not come into it at that moment. Kirstie was hurt! Her children had been in grave danger while she and Ethan had been having a leisurely coffee at the hospital.

He was ahead of her and called over his shoulder, 'Take it easy, Francine. We're going to have enough on our hands if Kirstie's injuries are serious, so save your strength for then.'

She nodded and slowed down, and by the

time she reached the first ambulance Ethan was standing by the doors with his arm around a white-faced Ben as the paramedics lifted the stretcher that held their daughter carefully onto the tarmac.

Kirstie was semi-conscious with a large gash on the side of her head where it must have struck something inside the bus when it had gone out of control, and as Francine took her limp hand in hers and hugged Ben to her with the other one, the ambulance crew began to wheel the stretcher through the main doors of A and E, with the three of them hurrying alongside.

Behind them was a procession of other young casualties on stretchers, some with parents and others, whose families didn't yet know about the accident, being comforted by nurses.

The most seriously injured was Dennis, the bus driver. He had taken the full impact of the falling tree inside the driver's cab and although now conscious was being X-rayed for a possible fractured skull and severe arm and shoulder injuries.

When the doctors had told him what Ben had done, he'd said weakly, 'It's a good job young Lomax was on board. What that kid doesn't know about auto engines isn't worth knowing.'

The doctor who came to see Kirstie arranged that X-rays be done of her head to check for a haematoma or brain damage, and for a fracture of her forearm. Ethan's face was grim as he listened to what the doctor had to say.

He could see Francine holding tightly onto Ben out of the corner of his eye, ashen with shock as she looked down at their precious daughter, and it felt like a lifetime since they'd been dawdling over their coffee.

It was a godsend that they had, otherwise they would have been on the way home while the ambulance had been bringing Kirstie to the hospital. What had happened to her and the other unfortunate youngsters on the bus made the problems that he and Francine had encountered over recent months seem as nothing by comparison. The welcome news about her continuing state of good health regarding the pregnancy had been blotted out by this.

Kirstie was fully conscious now and X-rays hadn't shown any internal bleeding or bruising of the brain from the head injury, but they'd shown the fracture of her arm that the doctor had suspected, and the deep cut on her head where she'd been thrown forward would need cleansing and stitching.

That wasn't all. There was another cause for concern. Weepy and hurting, Kirstie was saying she couldn't hear anything.

'Obviously there is some hearing loss, which could be temporary.' the doctor in A and E told them. 'It can happen after a severe blow to the head and can return once any perforation of the eardrum has healed, but we'll see what the audiology department has to say, and in the meantime the head wound will be cleaned and then stitched now that we know there is no internal bleeding.'

* * *

Audiology came up with the findings that there *was* a perforated eardrum and bruising of the ear canal on the left side and that during the next few days they would be checking progress, or lack of it, with regard to the problem sorting itself out. They were also told that when her arm had been put in a cast and the cut on her head stitched Kirstie would be taken up to the children's ward to be with the rest of those who had been hurt.

Thankfully none of the injuries appeared to be life threatening, but the bus driver's condition was causing anxiety amongst the hospital staff, his relatives and everyone connected with the school

Dennis was a nice old guy who'd been driving all his life with never a bump or fault in any shape or form. It had taken an old tree battered by the winds to fall and put an end to one of the pleasures of his later years, driving young ones to and from their school.

In the midst of it all a member of staff from the hospital reception desk in the main hall came to say that the press had arrived and were asking to interview Ben.

Ethan frowned at the thought, but Francine was watching Ben's cheeks reddening and eyes widening at the thought of it and said, 'Go with him, Ethan. Ben has something to be proud of. It would all have been so much worse if it hadn't been for his quick grasp of the situation. Let him have his special moment. I'll stay with Kirstie.'

'Yes, of course. You are right as always,' he told her heavily, but he had a smile for Ben. 'We have an amazing son.'

She wasn't always right, Francine reflected when they'd gone, and it wasn't what he really thought. Hopefully soon he might have cause to change his mind.

'They've taken my picture, Mum,' Ben cried when they came back, 'and it's going to be in the papers!'

'Yes, indeed,' Ethan agreed, looking slightly

less grim, and then went to try to explain to Kirstie what was happening, but she couldn't hear him, and he and Francine exchanged anxious glances.

Kirstie was settled in the ward now and feeling more cheerful in the company of some of her friends, yet still very upset about her hearing loss, and no way were they going to leave her for a moment unless they had to.

Ethan was on the point of taking Ben home and then coming back to join Francine for the night when Lucas appeared, having just come out of Theatre and heard about the accident.

'I'm due to leave for home shortly. I'll take Ben with me and he can sleep at our place for the night,' he offered, 'so that you two don't need to leave Kirstie.' He ruffled Ben's dark locks. 'I shall be wanting your autograph, and when Jenna hears about what you did she'll have lots of hugs for you.'

'She won't, will she?' he exclaimed in boyish dismay, and the two men laughed.

Ethan had been down to one of the hospital shops and bought a pad and pen so they could write everything down for Kirstie and that had cheered her up a little, but her head was aching from the injury, and her arm felt heavy and cumbersome from the cast they'd put on it.

When he looked around him it was clear that they were no different from any of the other parents whose children had been injured in various ways and didn't want to leave them under the circumstances.

'Can you imagine how it would have felt if you'd been in France when this happened?' he commented soberly, and watched her expression change from caring mother to that of chastised wife and quickly added, 'That was not meant as a criticism. It was just a comment. And will you please go into the parents' room at the end of the corridor and lie down for a while? You look exhausted.

'Kirstie has had some pain relief so may sleep the rest of the night once it kicks in, and you must try to do the same for both your sake and the little one's. I'll be around all the time if she needs either of us.'

'All right,' Francine agreed mechanically, and as she eased herself down onto a sofa that was for the use of visitors staying overnight she thought that however Ethan might have meant what he'd said, it was true. By cutting herself off from them for part of the time, as she had been doing, she could easily have not been there for Kirstie.

But it wouldn't have been like that if he had let her have her dream instead of leaving her to make it come true without him, and that had been a vain hope. It hadn't worked because without him she was nothing.

She hadn't admitted it to herself during the long months while they'd argued about her wanting to live in France, but since she'd got her wish and found it not to be as rewarding as she'd promised herself it would be, slowly but surely she was facing up to the fact that life without Ethan was no life.

If she loved him as much as she hoped he loved her, she should be willing to live with him in an igloo at the North Pole if need be.

Daylight brought with it some reassurance for most of the injured children and their families, but for Kirstie the hearing problem still prevailed and Ethan explained to her gently that it could be a few days before they saw any change.

Jenna arrived with Ben quite early. He'd been fretting to know how Kirstie and the other injured children were and, besides, she had to be at the surgery for half past eight.

She had a message from Barbara to deliver. 'Mum says to tell you how sorry she is to hear about the accident and hopes that Kirstie and all of those who were injured will soon be home. How is Dennis this morning, do we know?'

'Not as yet,' Ethan told her, 'but I popped into Intensive Care during the night and the nurses on duty said there was a slight improvement in his condition. His arm and shoulder were shattered from the impact of the tree and he'd been in Theatre for hours.'

When she was on the point of leaving he said, 'Put Leo in the picture, will you, Jenna? I've got my mobile with me in case he needs me for anything, and do tell your mother thanks for her message.'

'She's known Dennis for years.' she said sombrely as she reached for her car keys.

But Dennis wasn't out of danger yet as one of the parents who'd been to see him had just come back with the news that the injured bus driver had just had a heart attack.

Later in the morning they left Ben with Kirstie while they went for a quick bite and while they were waiting to be served Francine said, 'I was only catnapping during the night, you know. I saw you every time you came to check on me, so now what about some sleep for you?'

He shook his head. 'Not until the doctor has done his rounds. Leo has called from the surgery and everything is under control there. The district nurse who's filling in for Phoebe is off with a strained back, which as we both know goes with the job, but that is the only problem at the moment and she's hoping to be in tomorrow.'

Ethan's dedication to the practice would always be part of their lives. He would never want to give it up in a thousand years. she thought. She must have been insane to ever think he would.

They were back on the ward, the doctor was approaching, and everything else was forgotten as they listened to what he had to say after he'd examined Kirstie.

'I note that the hearing is no better,' was his first comment to Francine and Ethan. 'We must give the eardrum time to heal. It will be some weeks before the cast on the arm can be removed, but it should be as good as new. Let's take a closer look at the head wound.'

A nurse had taken off the bandaging in readiness for his visit and as he observed it keenly he pronounced, 'There doesn't appear to be any infection, but there might be a scar when it has healed properly and the stitches have been removed. If there is, we can decide what to do about it then.'

'We'll be keeping Kirstie in for a few days,' he told them. Glancing around the ward, he said, 'It would seem that she won't be short of company.'

By Thursday they were still going back and forth to the hospital to be with their daughter. But, they'd spent the night before at their respective houses at Kirstie's insistence because she was feeling much better.

Her head didn't hurt so much because it was healing and she'd got used to the cast on her arm. All they needed now was for her hearing to come back of its own accord.

Kirstie met them at the door of the ward, pushing a wheelchair that one of her school friends was using due to the leg fracture she'd received in the bus crash, and as they observed her cautiously Kirstie said, 'Say something, Mum.'

'Hello, my darling,' Francine said slowly.

'I heard you!' she cried. 'Not as loud as I'm used to, but I heard what you said. The doctor has been to see me and says I'm going to have another X-ray and if it shows that everything is all right inside my ear, I can come home!'

'Wonderful' Ethan said huskily. 'I have to go to the surgery but will be back shortly so don't go away, will you, Kirstie?'

He had to go to the surgery to keep a nine o'clock appointment with a patient who was dreading the results of tests that he'd had taken, and he wanted to be there as the man was a friend as well as a patient and had a disabled wife to cope with, who was not always the easiest of people to deal with.

Keith Balfour was already seated in the waiting room when he arrived, looking as if he was on a knife edge, and Ethan wasted no time in calling him into his consulting room.

'Tell it to me straight, Ethan,' Keith said

when he'd settled himself at the other side of the desk.

'Of course,' he told him. 'I would be doing you no favours if I didn't, Keith. Your count has gone up from seven to nine and a half, which is not good, but we're not panicking yet. If it had shot up to twenty there would be cause for concern, but you haven't reached that point yet. If you had we would be thinking about prostate cancer and it would be action stations, usually a strong blast of radiotherapy in an uncomfortable place.'

'Remember this, I'll be keeping a close watch on you, and the hospital will be sending you regular appointments for the urology clinic. So go home and don't let the worry of it get a stranglehold on you. Do I take it that Barbara and Jenna don't know you have this problem?'

'Yes, that's correct. I don't want Barbara to know because she relies on me so much, and I haven't told Jenna because these are precious days for her, the first months of her marriage and a baby on the way. I don't want to spoil them. Time enough to tell them both when and if I find I have something that has to be said, and you've put my mind at rest for the time being anyway.'

He'd endured a lifetime with Barbara which couldn't have been easy, knowing her, and wouldn't put the blight on his daughter's happiness by burdening her with the huge worry he was carrying around with him.

Comparing Keith and Henri, his French father-in-law whom he'd loved and respected, with his own father, who moaned and grumbled all the time, was like putting silk beside sackcloth.

After a quick chat with Leo he set off for the hospital once more to join Francine and Kirstie with hope in his heart, and on arriving called first to see Dennis, the bus driver, who had survived the heart attack and was slowly recovering from his injuries.

'Where's your lad, Dr Lomax?' he asked. 'He saved my life, you know, by stopping the bus. I shudder to think what would have happened to me and those youngsters if he hadn't.'

'Ben is back at school Dennis,' he told him. 'And now that you're feeling a little better, I know he'd love to come and see you.'

'Does he want to be a doctor like you?' he asked, and Ethan laughed.

'No, not at all. Ben's passion is for cars, and we're fairly sure he will pursue a career in that field in some form or other.'

When he arrived back at the ward Francine and Kirstie had just been given the results of the tests that Kirstie had had earlier, and although her hearing wasn't yet back to normal, the signs were there that it was returning, and she was being discharged with instructions to come back to see a consultant audiologist in a week's time for further checks.

It was midday. Francine and a happy Kirstie were back at Thimble Cottage and Ethan was about to go to the practice. On the point of leaving he was aware of Francine's pallor and the dark circles beneath her eyes and suggested that she go to bed for the afternoon with the assurance that he would make the evening meal.

'It is just stress that is making me look like this,' she said. 'I'll be fine now we have Kirstie home.' When he'd gone she went upstairs and phoned the solicitor who was acting for her in the divorce to request her to stop the proceedings.

She had already decided that the French dream was over, knew that was all it had ever been, and Kirstie being hurt had been another prod to her conscience. It had reminded her of the day when the vicar's wife had brought their son to her with the serious chest infection, and how when they'd gone she'd shuddered at the thought of not being there for a child of hers when she was needed. That could easily have been the case over the past week, but the fates had been kind.

She felt better after that and when Ethan arrived home in the evening after taking up the reins at the practice once more there was colour in her cheeks and a new sense of purpose in her expression.

CHAPTER EIGHT

IT WAS half-term at Ben and Kirstie's school and Ethan was happier than he'd been in a long time because his daughter's hearing had righted itself, the head injury was healing satisfactorily, and the only reminder of the accident was the cast on her arm, which most of her school friends had written on.

Added to his relief was the knowledge that Francine hadn't been across the Channel of late. He'd made no comment, been content to watch developments with spirits rising, until on the Friday night in the middle of the two-week break she'd said, 'Can we go back to our routine of you having the children for the weekend as you usually do when I'm away, and could you keep them with you for the rest of the week as well? It seems like a lifetime since I was in

France and as they're on holiday—' She'd seen his expression and her voice trailed away.

He'd been crazy to think she'd given up on it, he thought grimly. When he'd accused her of having it all sorted and fitting him into her life when it suited her, he hadn't been wrong. What a fool to think all the misery was going to go away because Francine hadn't been to Paris of late.

'Of course I'll have the children,' he'd said tightly. 'Some of us are contented with our lot. But not you, it would seem. I should have known better than to think you might have come to your senses.' To add to his annoyance he'd registered that she was smiling.

So she'd gone early on Saturday morning, this time not just with an overnight bag but with a sizeable suitcase, and fool that he was Ethan had taken her to the railway station to catch a London train as this time she was travelling to France by train to avoid flying in a state of advanced pregnancy, and he wanted to make sure she was safely on her way to get the London connection before he left her. But there were no fond goodbyes, just a peck on the cheek before she boarded the Paris train.

Inside the house that had been the cause of the disruption in their lives it was the same as always, the feeling of quiet emptiness as if it had been waiting for her, and she felt as if she wanted to go from room to room to tell it that it was going to have to be goodbye.

She'd come for a longer stay to arrange the inside as attractively as she could before she put it on the market, having decided that it needed to be out of her life completely if it couldn't be totally in it.

Once it was sold she wouldn't pine to live there any more. It would be the end of a chapter and a new beginning with Ethan.

It took all weekend to arrange it as she wanted, as well as Monday and Tuesday, and on the Wednesday she asked an estate agent in the centre of Paris to send someone give her a valuation on the assumption that if she was satisfied with it they could put it on the market.

When they'd been and gone she stood in the middle of the sitting room and wept. Yet she was at peace with herself for the first time in months, and for what was left of the week she spent the time seeing all the places that she loved especially, telling herself that she wasn't going to disappear from the face of the earth and neither was Paris.

She hadn't actually accepted the valuation on the spot, but once she was home and had considered it she would either consult another firm for comparison or tell the first one to go ahead. Soon it would be time to show Ethan where her loyalties lay.

That was her thought, until she arrived back in Bluebell Cove on the following Saturday morning to discover that her father-in-law had been hospitalised with a stroke and Ethan and the children were on their way to Bournemouth to see him. He'd left a note explaining the situation, and at the bottom had put:

If there is no real cause for alarm will be back before Monday morning as Ben and Kirstie are due back at school and I've got the practice to see to. As much as they love grumpy old grandpa, they won't want to miss the bonfire on Sunday night.

Lastly, as an afterthought, he'd written, *Hope you enjoyed France.*

She groaned. Just as she'd got to the point of putting everything right between them this had happened, and it stood to reason that Ethan wouldn't be thrilled at having to take Ben and Kirstie with him at such a worrying time, when if she'd been there he wouldn't have had to. Was she ever going to get anything right again? she thought as she picked up the phone to ring his parents' number in the hope that he would be there.

'I've just read your message,' she told him when he answered. 'I'm so sorry about your father. How bad is the stroke?'

'Not as bad as it might have been. Mum is with

him now. The children and I have just got back from the hospital,' he said in flat tones. 'I've spoken to the consultant on the stroke unit and he's anticipating partial recovery, but I can't see Dad being a good patient! Fortunately Mum is used to him and has plenty of stamina. We'll be leaving here Sunday lunchtime if there are no further concerns about him and hopefully will be back in time for the bonfire.'

'I'll have a meal ready,' she promised.

Into the pause that followed he said, 'No need. There'll be lots of food at the bonfire. How are you and the baby? You never phoned while you were there.'

'Neither did you,' she pointed out mildly.

'That might be because I haven't had a minute to spare. Francine, you didn't answer my question.'

'Both mother and child are fine. The new year is going to bring you joy, Ethan.'

She wasn't sure if he'd heard the last part of what she'd said as he was saying, 'I'll have to go. Mum has just come back from the hospital and I want to hear the latest about Dad.'

'Give her my love,' she said gently. Jean Lomax was a gem of a mother-in-law. They'd been good friends from the moment of meeting.

For the rest of the weekend Francine couldn't settle. She'd come back from France ready to tell Ethan that she was home to stay, and the moment had been postponed because of his absence and the reason for it.

The three of them arrived home late Sunday afternoon, as he'd hoped they might, and after she'd held Ben and Kirstie close she turned to Ethan, not expecting any warm embraces from that source after the way they'd parted at the railway station, but when their glances met there was warmth in his as he observed her and the child she was carrying.

She was back, the wife who had become a stranger with agendas of her own that she rarely shared with him. He hated her being alone in the French house, but at least when it was just for the weekend she was home almost as soon as she'd gone, but this time it had been a long and miserable week without her.

Yet thinking back to the first time she'd gone there without him and taken the children with her, a week was nothing compared to the months of separation then that had ended with her un-expected arrival in Bluebell Cove on Christmas Eve.

Soon the calendar would have gone full circle and another new year would be upon them with another child to love, and where would their relationship go from there?

'So how is your dad today?' she was asking, bringing his sombre thoughts back to the present.

'Improving. Some of the use has come back into his legs, which is where the stroke had the most effect, but it is early days. They won't be sending him home yet and I don't want them to, for my mother's sake.'

Ben and Kirstie were already upstairs, put-ting on warm clothes to keep them snug at the bonfire and anxious to be off to meet their friends, while Francine and Ethan followed at a slower pace, each with their thoughts in very different channels.

Food was on offer in the community centre just down the road, traditional fare such as parkin, hot soup, and chestnuts and potatoes roasted in the fire that was already glowing red, and all around them with its own special kind of warmth was the community feeling.

The local bobby was there, out of uniform but keeping a watchful eye on the proceedings, and a fire engine was parked not far away just in case, all part of the usual routine on Bonfire Night.

Something that wasn't expected was the arrival of Dennis, recently out of hospital and looking pale and drawn but with a smile on his face as he asked a couple of teenage girls, 'Is young Ben Lomax here?'

'Yes,' one of them told him. 'He's over there, kicking a ball about with his friends.'

'Would you mind asking him to come across? I want a word with him.'

'You're the driver on the school bus, aren't you?' the other girl said.

'Not any more. The tree that fell put paid to that,' he said wryly, and watched as they went to deliver his message.

When Ben heard who it was asking to see him he left what he was doing straight away. He'd been to see Dennis a few times in hospital and the elderly bus driver had really appreciated it. To discover that he was now back home with his family was great news.

'I've brought you something, laddie,' Dennis said when he came galloping up, and he presented Ben with a gift-wrapped parcel. 'It's to say thanks for what you did. Your parents must be very proud of you.'

'We are,' Ethan told him as he and Francine approached, delighted to see Dennis at the bonfire and curious to know why he was there.

A crowd was gathering, also curious, and when they saw Ben and Dennis together someone shouted, 'Three cheers for Ben Lomax, our local hero.' And having got used to being a celebrity, he bowed amidst the cheers.

When everyone had dispersed and gone back to their enjoyment of the night, Ben opened the parcel and gave a whoop of delight when he saw what was inside. Dennis had given him a collector's piece, a pewter desktop model of a Ferrari, and was smiling as he witnessed his young friend's pleasure.

After they'd chatted for a while Ben took him to the community centre for some food and a rest and Ethan said laughingly, 'If it goes on like this, our son won't be able to get a baseball cap to fit his head.' As Francine sparkled across at him it was a special moment of the kind that had become all too rare.

He ached with love for her and all the time wished he'd handled it better when the subject of them going to live in France had first cropped up. He'd once thought he must be the only man in the world who'd had to compete with a house for his wife's affections. Yet it applied both ways,

Francine coming second to a medical practice, or so she saw it.

In the light of the fire her face was indescribably beautiful with its fine bone structure and lovely green eyes. He hoped the baby she was carrying would have its mother's grace and attractiveness, as Kirstie and Ben did.

Jenna and Lucas were there and when they met up with them the two women were soon engrossed in baby talk and the men in medical matters.

From Lucas came a comment that he'd seen Barbara at his clinic a few days ago and she'd been in reasonable health considering the state of her heart and her debilitating rheumatoid arthritis.

'In fact, my mother-in-law was quietly content, happy almost,' he'd said 'and whatever the reason, I hope she'll be in the same frame of mind when her grandchild arrives.'

'You need have no doubts about that,' Ethan told him. 'Barbara will be over the moon when she and Keith become grandparents, and without my betraying a patient's confidence, keep an eye on Jenna's father, will you? He's the one with health problems at the moment, but doesn't want to worry his wife and daughter for the time being.'

When they strolled along to the community centre Leo was there, chatting to Lucy, the elderly practice nurse, and Ronnie, the lifeguard, who wasn't looking quite so bronzed in the chill of winter.

The Enderby family was also there and as Ethan chatted to the villagers who depended on him for their good health Francine thought with sudden wistfulness that she *was* doing the right thing in selling the house in France.

His happiness came first. The children were easy enough to please because they were only young, but Ethan's contentment was a different matter, and with regard to that there was the valuation she'd been given the week before. At the time it had seemed reasonable but having checked house prices on the Internet that morning before Ethan and the children had arrived home, she was regretting having only asked for one. Her parents wouldn't want her to sell their beautiful house for less than its worth.

The fact that she was selling it at all would be unexpected to everyone except herself, and come Monday morning she would arrange for other valuations to be done, with each property firm gaining access with the key that was in the keeping of her French solicitor.

It would delay telling Ethan of her decision for a little while longer, but she did want it to be already on the market when she told him, so that he would see just how much she was prepared to forget her dream.

Preparations for another Christmas in Bluebell Cove were under way as soon as Bonfire Night was past and with each reminder of it came the thought for both Francine and Ethan that soon their baby would be born into a new year shrouded in uncertainty.

One day in late November Ethan had a phone call from Barbara, asking him to stop by the first chance he got as there was something she wanted to discuss with him.

She gave no inkling of what it was and he was curious, as with complete confidence in him she never interfered with the practice—or his private life, for that matter, though she had been rather sour towards Francine when she'd come back to Bluebell Cove.

On the evening of the same day he went to Four Winds House and, leaving her husband to watch television, Barbara took Ethan into her study and once they were settled asked, 'Are you happy with your life, Ethan?'

He was observing her with raised brows and questioned, 'Why do you ask?'

'Because I care about you. I've watched you over past months and can see that you're pulled two ways by your dedication to the practice and your wife's longing to return home since she lost her parents.'

He sighed. 'That's true enough, Barbara, but where is all this leading? I don't think even you can suggest a solution.'

'Don't underestimate me,' she said with a dry laugh. 'I have a plan that might work to the satisfaction of you, me, Francine *and one other person.*'

He smiled. 'I'm afraid you've lost me.'

'Not for long, I promise. I can't tell you what it is at this moment but I should soon be able to and then it will be up to you. So will you trust me on this?'

'I've never had cause not to, have I?' he replied. 'So, yes, of course I'll trust you, though you've left me extremely curious.'

She was getting slowly and painfully to her feet, reaching for her stick and telling him, 'Like I say, it won't be for long, and now will you join us for a glass of wine? Keith and I usually indulge around this time.'

Later that evening he walked home thinking that maybe Barbara was cracking up, fantasising, but it was kind of her to be concerned about him and he put the strange conversation out of his mind and turned his thoughts to what the children had said they would like for Christmas. He wanted to give Francine something that would make her really happy, but so far hadn't thought of anything that was going to achieve that in the present climate.

The valuations she'd asked for were coming through slowly, too slowly, Francine felt, eager to let Ethan see how much she loved him. Some of them were higher than the first, others lower, and she was wishing she'd taken more care in getting the right selling price for the house before leaving it. There was just one left to come and then she would decide.

She was still working mornings at the surgery, against Ethan's wishes now that the pregnancy was so far advanced, but as she insisted that she felt fine and as it was flu vaccination time, he was going along with it.

Charlotte Templeton had popped in to tell her that the chemotherapy that the oncologist at the hospital had prescribed had resulted in some improvement of the Paget's disease. Francine had been able to reassure her that a report she'd received from them had confirmed that, and the popular headmistress had left with a lighter heart.

There'd been no further cryptic meetings with Barbara and Ethan's curiosity was dwindling as the silence from that direction confirmed his surmise that she was starting to be confused, even though she was the last person he would have ever expected it to happen to.

There had also been no recent weekends in France for Francine and he wondered why, but decided that the less it was mentioned the better, quite unaware that now the die had been cast Francine wasn't going to go back because it would hurt too much, even though the decision had given her the peace of mind she'd sought.

He was to find that he'd been wrong about Barbara with the razor-sharp mind. He'd done her an injustice by taking it for granted that her mind was failing. It was definitely not the case.

Another phone message had him calling again at the house on the headland and this time everything became clear, so clear that he was dumbstruck at the shrewdness of what she was suggesting.

'You know that when I had to retire you were the only person I could trust to take over from me, don't you, Ethan?' was her opening comment. He nodded and she went on to say, 'There is one other person who has my respect as much as you have, and that's my nephew Harry.

'Suppose he was available to take your place and by doing so could leave you free to live in France with your wife and family, how would you feel about that?'

'Are you telling me that Harry is leaving Australia to come back here?' he asked, his voice hoarse with amazement. 'Since when, Barbara?'

'Since he lost his wife in an accident. He's coming back to his roots and Francine wants to go back to hers, doesn't she?'

'Er, yes, she does,' he said slowly, as what she was suggesting sank in.

Harry Balfour had been a great guy when

they'd worked together in the practice in the old days as G.Ps with Barbara in charge. It would be good to see him again.

He'd married an Australian girl he'd met on holiday and had gone to live in Australia and practise medicine there, and now it seemed that sadness had come into his life.

'But would you be willing to make that sort of sacrifice?' she was asking.

'Yes, I would,' he said levelly. 'It wouldn't be a sacrifice if it made our marriage whole again. I've sometimes thought I'd like to do the same as Harry did, get involved in the medical side of things in another country. So is it definite that he's going to be free to take over?'

'Yes. I'm pretty sure. We've spoken at length about it, but I didn't want to involve you until I was certain. I'll speak to him again the first chance I get, but don't say anything to Francine until Harry has confirmed his intentions.'

As he walked home Ethan was in a daze. From the most unlikely source had come an answer to months of heart-searching and he couldn't wait to see Francine's face when he told her that her dream might be about to materialise. But before he said anything he had to be sure that Harry Balfour was available to take over the practice and that Kirstie and Ben would be happy to live in Paris permanently.

Francine had said she thought them saying they wanted to live in Bluebell Cove all the time was a ploy to get them all living together rather than reluctance to live in France. So he was going to have to make sure she was right. And that they would be as happy living there as they were here, *as long as he could promise them that both their parents would be there with them.*

He recollected that there had been plenty of friends on the scene near the French house when the three of them had surprised Francine by turning up unexpectedly that time, but he needed to hear from their own mouths what they thought about it as a permanent arrangement.

* * *

It was a week before he heard from Barbara again. It seemed that Harry had been out of town, visiting friends, and hadn't expected to hear from her so soon. The answer when it came was that he would love to take over the practice from Ethan and would be free of his commitments over there by the middle of January.

That meant a chat with the children was his first priority without a word to Francine who he knew, like himself, would put their happiness first.

If they had no problem with the move then would come the special moment when he would be able to tell her that he was ready to do what she'd asked him to do so many times, that the long wait was over.

It was Saturday morning and Kirstie and Ben were watching television when he went across to Thimble Cottage. He'd watched Francine drive off to do some shopping so he took the opportunity to put the question to them.

When he asked them if they would like to live

in France all the time they observed him doubtfully and, reading their expressions, he said, 'I
mean all of us.'

Ben was the first to speak in the silence that
followed the question. 'And would we go to
the same school where we went before?' he
questioned.

'I don't see why not,' he told him. 'We can
check on that.'

'Yes, then,' was the reply. 'We said we didn't
like it over there because we wanted to live with
you and Mum at the same time, but actually it
was just as great living there as it is living here,
wasn't it, Kirstie?'

'Yes, it was,' she agreed, 'but what does Mum
say?'

'She doesn't know yet, so please don't say
anything. I'm going to tell her tonight that I've
found someone to take charge of the practice
and that we're all going to live in Paris.'

The last valuation had arrived that morning.
Francine had made a decision on which to

choose and was going to ring the company first thing Monday morning to instruct them to put the house up for sale.

Now she could spring the big surprise on Ethan and watch the happiness on his face when he heard what she had to say. Tonight they would share the same bed, sleep in each other's arms with the little kicking one between them, and she would be content.

She rang him when she got back from the shops and said, 'Would you like to come over for dinner tonight?'

'I'd love to,' he told her, and hoped the children hadn't forgotten their promise not to say anything before they'd gone to the birthday party of one of their friends. They'd been invited to stay the night, which fitted in nicely with what he had planned, leaving Francine and him with the place to themselves.

When she opened the door to him it was clear that she'd dressed for the occasion, overdressed, he decided, if she didn't know what he'd come to say, in a flowing, gold-embroidered kaftan that concealed her pregnancy and with soft golden slippers on her feet.

On the other hand, *she* might think that *he* was acting a bit over the top. He'd brought her flowers, a huge bouquet of cream roses, and her surprise at the gesture told him that Francine knew nothing of what he had to tell her.

Yet when he saw the table set out with the best china and cutlery he wasn't so sure, and when the food she'd cooked turned out to be some of the French dishes that he loved he was even less sure.

When they'd finished the meal and were sitting by the fire with their coffee he cleared his throat. The moment had come that Francine had long waited for. He was about to show her what really came first in his life, and it wasn't the job.

She was placing her cup and saucer carefully onto the small table beside her and before he could speak she said softly, 'I have something to tell you that is very special, Ethan.'

'Go ahead, then,' he said evenly, and thought that whatever it was it couldn't be as 'special' as what he had to tell her. He wished he'd been able to have his say first.

'I'm putting the house in Paris on the market,' she was saying with eyes bright with the antici-pation of his delight. 'I'm accepting a valuation I've been given and am going to ring first thing Monday to instruct the company to undertake the sale of it.'

If she *was* expecting delight, she didn't get it.

'What? Why?' he cried. 'For goodness' sake, don't do that, Francine!'

'Why do you say that?' she asked blankly. 'Don't you understand? I can't hold out any longer. I need to be with you all the time, Ethan. Without you I might as well not exist.'

'I don't want you to come back here to live.' he continued in the same raised tone. 'You can't sell the house in France. You're going to need it.'

She was deathly pale. 'Are you telling me that

you have someone else to love—yes? Maybe it is Phoebe, eh? You concern yourself about her all the time.'

He groaned. 'There is no one else. There never has been. There never will be.'

'Yet you tell me I will need the house! Please go, Ethan. I was willing to give up my dream for you because I love you so, but it's too late for us. You don't want me any more, do you?'

She had one foot on the bottom of the stairs as he said in a low voice, 'You aren't the only one who will need the house, Francine, we all will. I'm resigning from the practice and we're going to live in France. So, you see, the dream isn't lost, it is alive and well.'

She turned slowly to face him, transfixed. 'It is what I have wanted so much,' she breathed, 'but I can't let you do that, Ethan. The practice is your life.'

He shook his head. 'No. *You* are my life, Francine.'

There were tears on her lashes. 'But who will take your place?' she choked. 'Leo hasn't been with you long enough, although he's good at the job, and the folks in Bluebell Cove won't take kindly to a stranger. They're used to having doctors that they know and can trust in charge of the practice.'

'And that is what they're going to get,' he told her with quiet satisfaction. 'It's sorted. Harry Balfour is coming back to the UK to live and wants to return to the life of a country G.P—in Devon.'

'I don't believe it,' she whispered.

He was smiling. 'You have to. The children are all for it. We had a chat this morning and you were right in what you thought. They are happy to live in either place as long as we're all together, and if you'll come closer I'll show how much of a one-woman man I am, then maybe you won't keep trying to fob me off onto Phoebe.'

CHAPTER NINE

WHEN the children were dropped home on Sunday morning they found their parents enjoying a leisurely breakfast at Thimble Cottage and in the hall was an assortment of suitcases.

'We're not going to France today, are we?' Ben cried.

'No, of course not,' Ethan told him. 'Your mother is moving back into our own house and inside the cases are her clothes and yours.'

'We are staying here in Bluebell Cove until after the baby is born,' Francine told them. 'And then we go to Paris to live. I am told that you are happy to go and am so delighted.'

It had been a magical night, Ethan was thinking as Kirstie and Ben perched on either side of her on the sofa. They'd made plans, made love, made promises they would keep for ever.

At one point he'd held her face tenderly between his two hands and looking deep into her eyes had said, 'The new life that is waiting for us both in France will be like sailing into calm waters after a storm, Francine. All we need now is the safe arrival of the other new life that you're carrying.'

Francine had been right when she'd said that the people in Bluebell Cove were accustomed to doctors that they knew as friends as well as representatives of the NHS, and when the news began to filter through that Ethan was resigning and leaving the village, there was much dismay.

Until reassurance came in the form of an announcement from the surgery explaining that Harry Balfour was coming back from Australia to take his place and everyone settled back into their previous contentment as there were not many who hadn't known and liked the man.

As for Ethan and his family, the villagers had only to look at him and his pregnant French wife to know that they were more than content with the future they were planning for themselves.

They'd been told that they would be most welcome to call if ever they were in Paris and it went without saying that call they would if the opportunity arose to catch up with the doctor who'd had all Barbara Balfour's dedication without her brittle outer shell.

The changeover at the surgery wasn't going to take place until mid-January. The baby was due in the new year and Francine wanted the birth to stay as planned in the same hospital that Kirstie and Ben had been delivered in.

Harry was not expected to arrive in Bluebell Cove until near the end of January, which suited Francine and Ethan as it meant they would be around for his parents over Christmas and New Year in case they were needed, though his father's condition was much improved to the relief of all concerned, including his wife, *especially his wife*!

'We might find ourselves a place over there when Grandpa is a little better,' Jean had said when she'd heard they were moving across the Channel.

'Not too near you, yet not too far away.'

Her son and daughter-in-law had welcomed the idea as that really would be all the family together in the same place if Ethan's father's health caused any further problems.

To their parents' relief and the children's approval, the school near Paris had confirmed that they would re-admit Kirstie and Ben as soon they were settled in the area and the formalities had been dealt with, removing the last cloud in their sky as far as Ethan and Francine were concerned.

As winter tightened its grip on Bluebell Cove, with frosty mornings and hazy sunshine replacing autumn's glorious golden days, the four of them settled down to await the promises of the new year, and in the meantime gave their energies to the coming Christmas.

Francine and Ethan had gone shopping one Saturday for things for the baby and Christmas presents for Ben and Kirstie.

Their first call was to the nursery department in one of the large stores where an abundance of the kind of things they needed was on display, cribs. baby baths and clothes to mention a few items, and as they strolled from counter to counter, holding hands, she said softly, 'I can't believe we're doing this, Ethan, shopping for our extending family. I'm so happy I could burst.'

'Me too,' he replied. 'Every time I move in the night and feel you beside me it's magic, Francine, so wonderful that it's scary.'

When they'd bought for the child yet to come and arranged for delivery of their purchases, they went to buy for the children already in their lives. Ben had asked for a guitar as his main Christmas present and Kirstie was coveting a pink mobile phone.

When they'd finished shopping and were going back to the car Ethan said, 'I want to give you something really special as my Christmas gift. Is there anything you would like that I don't know about?'

'Not a thing,' she told him. 'You've already given me the most precious gift of all by giving up the practice to make my dream come true. I know how much that has cost you, Ethan, without you ever having to put it into words.'

He smiled down at her. 'There is no price on what I've done. The opportunity came out of the blue and I grasped it before it disappeared.' With his gaze on where the baby lay warm and secure inside her, he added, 'I'm not the only one with precious gifts to offer, am I?'

There was activity at the church as they drove by on their way home and they went in to find the vicar's wife and helpers getting it ready for the coming season with holly and other fresh greenery gracing the window sills, a nativity scene at the front and a Christmas tree tastefully decorated at the end of one of the aisles.

As they exchanged cheerful greetings the vicar's wife said, 'We have just had Jenna and Lucas here, and if their baby arrives in time for the Sunday before Christmas, she's going to let us place it in the crib when we do the nativity play. Won't that be lovely?'

Ethan was laughing as they left the church and when she asked what the joke was he said, 'I can't see Lucas being happy about his newborn lying in that old crib. It's been around for years gathering dust. If the baby arrives in time, just watch—it will be in its mother's arms instead of the crib.'

The first of the children that Jenna had promised Lucas on their wedding night was due a couple of weeks before Christmas, so there *was* a chance that it might be the star performer in the nativity play, with its mother taking second place dressed in the familiar blue robes that came out of storage each year for the event.

After much discussion Francine had persuaded Ethan to agree to them keeping the house in Bluebell Cove for coast and countryside breaks amongst old friends and acquaintances. He had been of a mind to sell it and make a clean break, but she had reasoned that although they were moving to France, a part of all four of them, him in particular, would always belong in Devon.

He'd originally wondered if Harry would be interested in either buying or renting their house, but before he'd had the chance to mention it to him the other man had asked if either of the apartments above the surgery was vacant and when Ethan had told him that one of them was, having not yet approached Leo about it, Harry had said that would suit him fine.

When he'd told Francine about the arrangement she'd said, 'But weren't you going to offer it to Leo after agreeing that Phoebe could rent the other one?'

'Yes, I was,' he'd replied, 'but he seems happy enough where he is for now. Harry does need to have somewhere he can move into straight away when he arrives and both apartments *are* furnished. I don't want to leave any loose ends when we've gone.'

If Christmas hadn't been in the offing, the days would have dragged to the birth of their child, which would be followed by their exodus across the Channel. But there was so much to do getting ready for the festivities and planning the next two big events in their lives that December seemed to be moving along fast, and as each day came Francine thought thankfully how different this Christmas was going to be from the last when she'd arrived without invitation, desperate to see her children and facing a new year that had held little promise of peace between Ethan and herself.

But the love they had for each other had triumphed in the end and brought reason and understanding into their lives. One day soon she was going to thank Barbara for her farsightedness and understanding. With the shrewdness that was so much a part of her she'd shown the two men that she cared for deeply the way ahead for each of them.

Jenna had given birth to a beautiful little girl they'd named Lily and been home from hospital a couple of days later, which had meant that the vicar's wife was going to get her wish on the Sunday before Christmas Day. A real live baby for the nativity scene held in her mother's arms instead of lying in the crib, as Ethan had prophesied.

It would soon be their time for rejoicing, Francine had thought that day as they'd walked home from the church, and tuning into her thoughts Ethan had said, 'Our cup runneth over, doesn't it?'

'It does indeed,' she'd replied.

There'd been the dancing through the village on Christmas Eve again, though now they were onlookers instead of part of the throng. It was followed by the Enderbys' ball at Wheatlands Farm and it was there that Francine found the opportunity to speak to Barbara when the other woman was alone for a moment.

'Thank you for making it possible for Ethan to resign from the practice with an easy mind Dr, Balfour,' she said. 'I'm so happy I can't believe it, though I do wonder how much he's hurting inside.'

Barbara's wintry smile came into view. 'He was hurting more when he was without you,' she said, and thought if anyone was hurting it was herself, but only she knew that.

As Christmas Day had passed with contentment on all sides Francine and Ethan were not to know that the road to happiness had an unexpected diversion ahead that was going to throw them way off track.

It was on the morning of Boxing Day when Francine started with early labour pains while the children were still asleep and she and Ethan were having breakfast. She gave a sudden gasp of pain and he was by her side in an instant.

'What is it?' he asked urgently.

'It is gone now, but it was like a contraction,' she told him. 'Maybe it will come again but I hope not. It is too early, Ethan, three weeks too early. The other two were late so it can't be. Aagh! It is there again.'

'Those are pretty fast contractions if they're labour pains.' he said. 'I'm taking you to the maternity unit at Hunter's Hill, Francine. We'll see what they have to say.

'Let's go. I'll pop upstairs to tell Kirstie and Ben what's happening and to stay put until they hear from us, and will bring your case down. Having it ready packed was a good idea.'

'I'm not sure if it was or not,' she commented glumly as they drove along deserted roads towards the town. 'Maybe I've wished this on myself by being too organised, or perhaps we shouldn't have been taking it for granted that nothing could touch us now.' As another contraction gripped her she subsided into silence.

Ethan was observing her anxiously. The sooner they got to the hospital the better. At that moment Francine cried, 'It is coming, Ethan! We are not going to get there in time.' He increased speed.

At that moment a cruising police car stopped in front of them and pulled him over. 'You were speeding, sir,' one of the uniformed officers told him. What's the rush?'

'This is the rush!' he cried, pointing to Francine. 'My wife is going to give birth any second and I'm going to need your assistance.'

'What? To deliver it?' the policeman said, taking a step back at the thought.

Ethan was helping Francine into the back seat and laying her gently across the cushions to examine her and he called over his shoulder, 'No. I'm going to take charge of the delivery. I'm a doctor.'

'OK,' was the reply. 'Just tell us what you want us to do and we'll do it.'

He saw immediately that she was right. The baby's head was already visible. 'Please tell me I can push!' she begged. 'I don't think I can hang on any longer.'

He was grabbing a towel that they always kept on the ledge above the back seat in case any of them went into the sea unprepared, and putting it in position he said gently. 'Push as hard as you like, Francine.'

She did and seconds later he told her, 'We have a son, Francine. Henri has arrived.'

'Is he all right?' she asked anxiously. 'The speed of his arrival hasn't hurt him?'

'He is perfect,' he assured her. 'And now we need to get you to hospital. The placenta needs to come away, but hopefully it will wait until we get there.'

'Let me see him first,' she said, and he held up a crying infant for her to feast her eyes on, and then wrapped him in the towel.

They were in the delivery room at the hospital after following the police car with its siren blaring in the peaceful Boxing Day morning. Staff had been waiting for them after receiving a message from the two officers to say that a mother and newborn baby were on their way.

Henri had been cleaned up by one of the nurses and the obstetrician in charge had declared him to be the equivalent of full term with his arrival having been so near the due date, but they would keep a close watch on him for any signs of distress.

The placenta had come away easily enough and all would have been well except for one thing. Francine was bleeding heavily. There was cause for alarm.

'It would seem that we have a postpartum haemorrhage here,' the obstetrician said. 'It could be due to a tear where the placenta was attached to the uterus, or because the uterus isn't contracting as it should be after the delivery. Or it could be because part of the placenta is still attached to the womb. Whatever the cause, your wife is going to need a transfusion and is going down to Theatre while we sort out what the problem is.'

Ethan nodded mutely. They were in the middle of a ghastly nightmare he thought as he looked down at Francine's pale face. There was fear in the beautiful green eyes looking up into his, but her voice was calm as she said, 'Take care of our children, Ethan, if anything happens to me.'

He took her hand in his and, kissing her soft palm, said, 'That goes without saying, my darling, but they're going to sort this out. Nothing is going to happen to you. It can't be allowed to. I won't let it.'

Before she could reply her bed was being wheeled towards the corridor and speechless with anxiety he walked beside it for as far as he could then stood back helplessly as they took her into the theatre.

When he arrived back on the maternity unit, Kirstie and Ben were gazing in wonder at the baby. Lucas had brought them, having seen their parents' hurried departure and gone to investigate, and they were wanting to know whether it was a boy or a girl as there were no visible signs to indicate its sex. He managed a smile and told them, 'You have a little brother.'

'Wow!' Ben cried, while Kirstie beamed her delight. She wasn't bothered either way as long as it was a baby to cuddle. But Kirstie being Kirstie, she wanted to know, 'So, where is Mum?'

'She's with the doctor and won't be long,' he told her, not meeting his daughter's clear gaze.

'What's wrong?' Lucas asked in a low voice when she'd turned away. 'You look like death.'

'Francine is haemorrhaging,' he told him raggedly. 'They've taken her down to Theatre to try and find the cause.'

His friend observed him sombrely. 'That's not good. When the children have had their fill of gazing at the baby I'll take them home to our place for as long as need be.'

'Thanks,' he choked, and wondered how long 'need be' might turn out to be.

Lucas and the children had gone, reluctantly on Ben and Kirstie's part, but there was no way Ethan wanted them to be there when Francine came out of Theatre. He didn't know how she would be, what state she would be in, and Kirstie in particular would be heart-broken to see her seriously ill.

When they'd departed he settled himself to wait, seated beside the baby's cot in a small side ward. As he looked down at his newborn son he thought achingly that the little red faced scrap lying there had no idea what his unexpected arrival had caused.

The minutes ticked by, each one like an hour, and it was as if everything else in his life was far away. Bluebell Cove, the practice, Paris and the elegant house that they'd been hoping to move into soon were all minor matters compared to what was happening to Francine.

It was incredible that having been without a single problem all the time she'd been pregnant, this should happen, he thought grimly. Yet post-partum haemorrhage *was* known to occur after a birth. It was always serious. Before improved methods of treatment had been introduced it had often resulted in the death of the mother.

The waiting came to an end in the early afternoon when the consultant obstetrician appeared and informed him that Francine was out of Theatre and in the high-dependency unit.

'And the bleeding?' Ethan asked.

'Hopefully sorted,' he said. 'There was a tear where the placenta had been attached to the uterus, and when that had been dealt with under general anaesthetic, the haemorrhaging stopped. Your wife has lost a lot of blood but the transfusions we've given her will replace that. You can go to see her whenever you like.'

He looked down at the baby and said, 'So this is the little guy who is the cause of all the trouble? Still, I bet if I asked his mother how she felt about it she would say it was all worth it as long as he's arrived safely.'

'You are right about that,' Ethan told him as his nerves began to feel not quite so knotted, and they went down to the high-dependency unit together, leaving a nurse in charge of little Henri.

Francine was still under the anaesthetic when they got there and as he gazed down at the woman he loved, who had been more concerned about her children than herself when in dire distress, tears choked him.

Thankfully the skills of people like themselves who cared about the well-being of others had brought her back from the brink of something too unbearable to contemplate. Soon she would be coming out of the anaesthetic with the bleeding controlled and her life saved because she'd been in the right place at the right time.

In keeping with that sentiment, the obstetrician was saying, 'We will be keeping both mother and baby in until I'm satisfied that your wife is recovering without any further complications. There shouldn't be any as the tear from where the placenta separated from the uterus has been repaired, along with a smaller tear of the cervix, and if the baby is here with her, it will be convenient for her to breastfeed him if she feels well enough once she moves to the maternity ward.'

His buzzer was bleeping. 'I have to go, I'm afraid, Dr Lomax, but rest assured I'll be keeping an eye on them both.' And before Ethan could express his heartfelt thanks, he was striding off to whatever awaited him next.

'The baby, Ethan, is he all right?' were Francine's first slurred words as she tried to focus on him when she came round after the anaesthetic.

'He's fine,' he told her gently. 'They're going to bring him to you in a little while.'

'Have the children seen him yet?'

'Yes, Lucas brought them and now he's taken them home with him. I've kept what was happening in Theatre from them. They've stopped the bleeding. It *was* caused by a tear when the placenta came away.'

'So what happens now?' she wanted to know. 'Will they let me go home?'

'Not just yet. They will be keeping you in for a few days until they're satisfied you're back to normal and that there will be no risk of any further bleeding, which is unlikely now that the problem has been dealt with. And Henri will be with you soon.

'Bringing him into the world in the back of the car was a nightmare, but seeing him appear whole and healthy was fantastic. What a Christmas present! He might have been a day late with it—after all gifts had been given—but we can forgive him that, can't we?'

'We can forgive him anything, anything at all,' she said weakly, and as another doctor appeared at that moment and the screens were pulled around the bed, Ethan held her hand while the medic examined her.

When he'd finished he gave a satisfied nod and told them that soon she would be moved to the ward and in a few days' time another scan would be done to make sure that all was well before she was sent home.

Lucas came back with the children shortly after she'd been moved to the ward and when he saw her lying there with the baby in a basinet beside her he said, 'Thank God, Francine! This poor guy has been going out of his mind with anxiety, and I've never seen my mother-in-law so distraught before.'

'Barbara might have engineered it so you could all move to France, Ethan, but you are still her blue-eyed boy, and I think everyone in Bluebell Cove must have been on the phone after I got home from here this morning, wanting to know how Francine was.'

She flashed Ethan a tired smile. 'I had to come through it. I couldn't leave you free to marry Phoebe.' And as Lucas observed them questioningly they laughed at what he decided must be a private joke.

It was evening, the children had gone home with Lucas once more as the nurses on the ward had said that their patient needed rest and quiet for twenty-four hours, and only Ethan remained beside the bed.

Francine was sleeping normally and one of the night nurses came up and said, 'Why don't you go home for a few hours, Dr. Lomax? It is what your wife would want you to do, get some rest.' After being given a promise that they would be in touch immediately if any problems should arise, he did what she'd suggested and went home.

When he arrived back in Bluebell Cove he didn't go to collect Ben and Kirstie straight away and didn't switch on any lights. He needed a few moments to himself and stood looking out of the window into the dark night, letting the quietness of the empty rooms calm his shattered nerves.

He could see the lights twinkling on the big Christmas tree in the square and it seemed incredible that it was still there, that the season wasn't over and New Year had yet to come. It was as if he'd been on another planet ever since Francine had felt that first contraction.

The last twenty-four hours had shown him beyond doubt that happiness was not to be taken for granted, no matter how hard it had been to come by, and he sat down and wept at the thought of how nearly it had been lost to them.

Take care of our children, Francine had begged when she hadn't been sure what lay ahead. He would care for them all with humble gratitude for the rest of his life, he thought. Nothing would ever change that, and with his composure returning and the nightmare of the last two days receding he switched on the lights, closed the curtains and decided that the three of them were going to have an early night so that he could be at the hospital promptly the next morning. Satisfied that things were definitely on the up, he went to collect his two elder children from the house next door.

Before he called it a day he rang Leo at the guest house. The surgery was due to reopen the following morning after the Christmas break and Ethan just wanted a quick word to put him in the picture with what was happening in his life as at the moment the practice seemed far away.

After receiving Leo's assurances that he was all geared up for whatever the coming morning brought at the surgery, and answering his concerns regarding Francine, Ethan went slowly up the stairs to bed.

EPILOGUE

FRANCINE and the baby were home. Henri was thriving and she was gradually recovering from the biggest scare she'd ever had. Kirstie was displaying nursing skills far beyond her years. Ben hovered awkwardly and disappeared fast when it was time for the baby to be changed, but kept going to look at him when no one was around, while Ethan was in a constant state of thankfulness as he watched over them all.

It was that same thankfulness that made him tell Francine what had been in his mind ever since he'd brought her home from hospital with little Henri.

She was propped up against the pillows in the middle of the night, feeding him, and Ethan was beside her with his arm around her shoulders when he said, 'There is something I'd like us to do before we leave here, Francine.'

'What?' she asked, smiling across at him, and he thought tenderly that neither of them had stopped smiling since she'd opened her eyes that day at the hospital.

When he didn't reply she asked laughingly, 'Do you want us to arrange to have a band playing ìLa Marseillaiseî when we board the plane, or request that the French President to be there to greet us when we arrive at the other end?'

'No,' he replied, laughing with her, 'though I won't say that the occasion doesn't warrant it.' Serious now, he explained, 'If you are agreeable, I'd like us to take our wedding vows again. You were always precious to me beyond compare and since I nearly lost you I feel as if I have to tell the world how much I love you. So what do you say, Francine?'

'I say yes, of course,' she said softly, and wondered if anyone in the medical encyclopaedias had ever burst with happiness. 'Suppose you ask the vicar if we can renew our vows during the last service of our time here?'

'Will I be able to be a bridesmaid?' Kirstie wanted to know, and was disappointed to hear that it wasn't that sort of occasion but that they were asking everyone back to the house afterwards for a celebration.

That made the event sound more appealing to the would-be bridesmaid and as Kirstie's thoughts veered in another direction she decided that it would be a good opportunity to show everyone how good she was at looking after little Henri.

Typical of Ben, he saw it merely as an occasion where there would be lots of food to eat, while dodging being patted on the head by elderly ladies, and hoped that some of his friends would be there.

When consulted, the vicar had said he was delighted to agree to their request and in the discussion that had followed they'd arranged for Henri's christening to follow the renewal of their wedding vows on the Sunday morning before they flew to France on the following day.

Jenna and Lucas had been asked to be his godparents, even though the two families would be separated by distance, but as they all agreed, France wasn't that far away and they would visit whenever the opportunity presented itself.

Harry had been in touch with Barbara again and also with Ethan. It seemed that there were some last-minute problems regarding the sale of his property that he didn't want to leave unsorted before leaving Australia and he wouldn't be arriving in Devon to take over the practice until a couple of days after they'd left.

It was a disappointment as Ethan had been looking forward to meeting him again and wanted to leave Bluebell Cove with the knowledge that the new doctor was already in place.

But at least Harry hadn't changed his mind—in fact, he seemed keener than ever—and once their French flight was airborne that would be it, the end of an era as far as he was concerned.

* * *

One evening when the children were out and they had the place to themselves, apart from Henri sleeping peacefully in his cot, Francine said, 'I sometimes wake up and think us going to live in France is just a dream.'

'It is no dream,' he told her softly. 'It is meant to be. I never thought it could be until the day that Barbara told me that Harry was coming back and everything fell into place. I can be a doctor in France just as here, so that's no problem, and if your mum and dad are looking down on us, they'll be highly delighted to know that, much as they liked Bluebell Cove, we are moving into their house, with me practising medicine French style, the children going to French schools, and the daughter they loved alive, well and content.'

'I don't deserve you,' she choked.

'Agreed. You deserve someone better,' he told her whimsically.

'That could be difficult,' she told him from the circle of his arms, 'because you are the best.'

* * *

The church was full on the January morning when they went to renew their marriage vows and have their child baptised. For Francine and Ethan the two ceremonies taking place at the end of their time in Bluebell Cove would create a bond that would never be broken, an occasion that would always have a special place in their hearts.

As they stepped forward to face the vicar, passing Henri to a proud Kirstie while they renewed their vows, there was total silence in the old village church for a few seconds then the bells began to ring out, as Ethan had arranged they should, and as they pealed joyfully up above in the bell tower the two of them, looking into each other's eyes, repeated the words they had said on their wedding day.

It had been a long time ago. They'd been head over heels in love then, and that same love was there still, stronger than before because it had been tested and tried more than they could ever have thought it would be, and it had triumphed.

Behind them Jenna was carefully relieving Kirstie of the baby in readiness for the christening, and Lucas was passing their beautiful little Lily to a proud Keith while he fulfilled his role as godfather to Henri. And there was a surprise for Ethan's grumpy father, sitting in a pew near the front with his patient wife, when the baby was baptised Henri Lawrence Lomax.

Back at the house where a meal had been laid on the atmosphere was a mixture of happiness and sorrow. A lot of people were going to miss Ethan Lomax and his family, not least Barbara who had actually been seen to wipe a tear from her eye, and no matter how good a doctor her nephew Harry was, the general feeling was that his predecessor was going to be a hard act to follow.

They were flying to France the following day and various crates containing household articles would be following them, but the furniture and curtains would be staying in position as there

was a fully furnished house awaiting them at the other end.

When all the people who had joined them after the church service had left, Francine and Ethan left the baby with his grandparents and went for a last walk along the seashore. There was a winter sunset on the horizon and the feel of snow in the air, and as they walked with arms entwined Barbara watched them from her sitting-room window and a smile replaced the tears of earlier in the day.

The next morning at the airport there was a crowd to wave them off, Jenna and Lucas with Lily, Barbara and Keith Balfour, all the staff from the surgery, the Enderbys, Charlotte the headmistress, Ronnie and his family. Meredith from the guest house was also there, and many more villagers who were feeling the same as Ethan was, that it was the end of an era with a new beginning in view.

When they reached the top of the walkway that led to the inside of the plane, with Kirstie

and Ben leading the way and Ethan bringing up the rear with Henri in his arms, Francine turned to him and said in a low voice, 'This is it, Ethan. We'll be airborne very soon—are you sure you want this? There is still time to change your mind.'

'Yes, I am sure,' he told her gently. 'I'm sure that this is the way we were meant to go. What do I have to do to convince you, Francine? Shout it from the top of the Arc de Triomphe or wear a beret? Come here while I kiss you into believing me.'

And as he did just that there was a round of applause from the cabin crew and they took the first step into their new lives.